Lifehouse

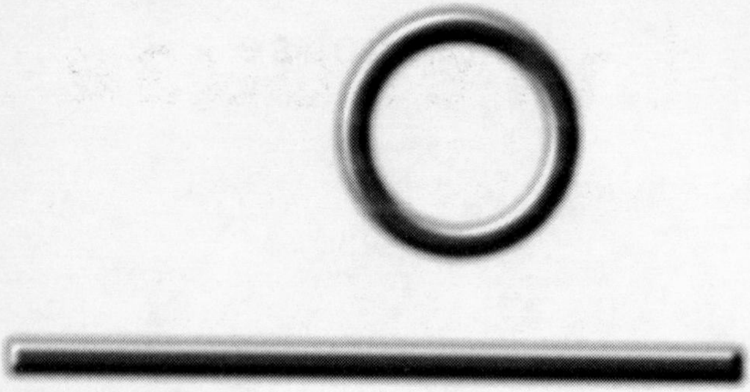

Lifehouse

By Pete Townshend

Adapted for radio by Jeff Young

Pocket Books

First published in Great Britain by Pocket Books, 1999
An imprint of Simon & Schuster UK Ltd
A Viacom Company

10 9 8 7 6 5 4 3 2 1

Simon & Schuster UK Ltd
Africa House
64-78 Kingsway
London WC2B 6AH

Simon & Schuster Australia
Sydney

A CIP catalogue record for this book is available from the British Library

ISBN 0-743-40845-4

Logo facing title page © Laurence Sutherland

Typeset in 11½ on 14pt Garamond
Design and page make-up by Peter Ward

Printed and bound in Great Britain by
Caledonian International Book Manufacturing, Glasgow

The **lifehouse** play was developed for radio by BBC Radio Drama in collaboration with Eel Pie. The first broadcast worldwide took place on 5 December 1999 exclusively on **BBC** RADIO 3 and the recorded version is published by BBC Worldwide and Eel Pie.

The play was directed and produced for the BBC by Kate Rowland, with the following cast:

Ray	David Threlfall
Sally	Geraldine James
Mary	Kelly Macdonald
Hacker	Shaun Parkes
Caretaker	Charles Dale
Rayboy	Phillip Dowling

The co-producer for Eel Pie was Tom Critchley.

introduction

For twenty-nine years I have been entangled in this thing called lifehouse. I blamed the frustration it caused me on its innate simplicity and my innate verbosity; one cancelled out the other. The story contained ideas that were once regarded as overly ambitious. I felt like a jungle explorer who had stumbled upon an Inca temple of solid gold and become impeded by roots and vines in a knot of undergrowth, only yards from civilisation. One day I would emerge crying aloud that I'd discovered something marvellous, but would be patted on the head and indulged in my triumphant ranting. The playscript you hold in your hands today is the result of this awkward, though not particularly heroic, journey. I have come to the end of a creative adventure in which I struggled as much to overcome my own impatience as obstacles in my path. I present you now with a finished play.

My allies in this satisfactory moment are many, but chiefly here I look to Jeff Young who adapted the story as a play for radio during our many creative brainstorms, and my BBC producer Kate Rowland who contributed so much more than a commission and – by my standards – some rather modest BBC money to contrast the rest of the magnificent traditional BBC resources provided. My creative facilitator and co-producer Tom Critchley was also vital to the process. I should also thank my old friend John Fletcher who worked with me on a substantial earlier draft for this BBC play, eventually retiring in frustration, telling me that I kept changing my mind. I simply enjoyed what had become a habitual process of exploration. I certainly enjoyed his company. One thing John did deliver for me was my sense of myself as a complete composer. At one time he compared me to Purcell, because of my quintessential Englishness rather than my skill with choristers, but it gave me the confidence to pursue the chamber orchestral drafts which were completed by Sara Loewenthal and Rachel Fuller and appear in the play – my first orchestral composition. Everyone in this creative team worked tirelessly and successfully to unravel the chief enigma presented by my original naive film script, which is whether the story is about anything interesting, or just about someone who used to be a really big rock star called Pete Townshend.

Because the script I wrote for Universal Pictures in 1971 was never realised as a film, or any kind of theatrical narrative drama, I have often found myself telling and retelling the story of **Lifehouse**, usually in conversation with interested journalists. John Fletcher believes it has evolved too much and become confused over the years purely because I have a needy celebrity's need to keep journalists engaged. But because the story itself is about a highly technological media corrupted by myopic conglomerates, many writers – working for 'the media Man' – have identified with my phobias about the future.

Briefly, the story of Lifehouse as it was presented to The Who in 1971.

A self-sufficient, drop-out family group farming in a remote part of Scotland decide to return South to investigate rumours of a subversive concert event that promises to shake and wake up apathetic, fearful British society. Ray is married to Sally, they hope to link up with their daughter Mary who has run away from home to attend the concert. They travel through the scarred wasteland of middle England in a motor caravan, running an air-conditioner they hope will protect them from pollution. They listen, furtively, to old rock records which they call 'Trad'. Up to this time they have survived as farmers, tolerated by the government who are glad to buy most of their produce. Those who have remained in urban areas suffer repressive curfews and are more-or-less forced to survive in special suits, like space-suits, to avoid the extremes of pollution that the government reports.

These suits are interconnected in a universal grid, a little like the modern Internet, but combined with gas-company pipelines and cable-television-company wiring. The grid is operated by an imperious media conglomerate headed by a dictatorial figure called Jumbo who appears to be more powerful than the government that first appointed him. The grid delivers its clients' food, medicine and sleeping gas. But it also keeps them entertained with lavish programming so highly compressed that the subject can 'live out' thousands of virtual lifetimes in a short space of time. The effect of this dense exposure to the myriad dreamlike experiences provided by the controllers of the grid is that certain subjects begin to fall apart emotionally. Either they believe they have become spiritually advanced, or they feel suffocated by what feels like the shallowness of the programming, or its repetitiveness. A vital side-issue is that the producers responsible for the programming have ended up concentrating almost entirely on the story-driven narrative form, ignoring all the arts unrestrained by 'plot' as too complex and unpredictable, especially music. Effectively, these arts appear to be banned. In fact, they are merely proscribed, ignored, forgotten, no longer of use.

A young composer called Bobby hacks into the grid and offers a festival-like music concert – called The Lifehouse – which he hopes will impel the audience to throw off their suits (which are in fact no longer necessary for physical survival) and attend in person. 'Come to the Lifehouse, your song is here'.

The family arrive at the concert venue early and take part in an experiment Bobby conducts in which each participant is both blueprint and inspiration for a unique piece of music or song which will feature largely in the first event to be hacked onto the grid.

When the day of the concert arrives a small army force gathers to try to stop the show. They are prevented from entering for a while, the concert begins, and indeed many of those 'watching at home' are inspired to leave their suits. But eventually the army break in. As they do so, Bobby's musical experiment reaches its zenith and everyone in the building, dancing in a huge dervish circle, suddenly disappears. It emerges that many of the audience at home, participating in their suits, have also disappeared.

There is no dramatic corollary. I didn't try to explain where they may have gone, or whether they were meant to be dead or alive. I simply wanted to demonstrate my belief that music could set the soul free, both of the restrictions of the body, and the isolating impediments and encumbrances of the modern world.

* * *

Sixties rock achieved so much in its first seven years, a period that to me now seems such a short space of time. My expectations of the rock form, The Who group, its managers and myself, were huge. During the development of **lifehouse**, my Svengali-like manager Kit Lambert suffered a massive spiritual demise and took refuge variously in the gloom of a famously cursed palazzo in Venice or the headiness of a Central Park hotel in Manhattan. While this was happening, the emotional distance of the otherwise encouraging Hollywood establishment confused me. I had written a script, which Universal Pictures had read and apparently understood: they had promised me two million dollars. Then there was silence. I came up against my first real brick wall since I had started writing and acting as spokesman for The Who and many in their audience. Until then I had felt omnipotent, I hope not arrogantly. But that wall that rose up between me and my **lifehouse** film stood up to every energetic idea I threw at it. I could not work out what to do.

Had I been working in theatre I believe I would have been encouraged to carry on, instructed that dramatic ideas need to be work-shopped and nurtured, not simply tossed onto paper and then talked, hyped (or sung) into being by the author. Chris Stamp, one of The Who's managers during the period in which *Tommy* was recorded, remembers a truly synergetic and symbiotic process of creativity then, something that for various reasons failed to happen when I presented **lifehouse** to The Who. I should say quickly that the band members and everyone involved were immensely supportive. The music I'd written with the script was excellent, and there was a lot of it. And not everyone found the story confounding.

Frank Dunlop was director of the brand new Young Vic theatre at the time, and through our meeting at AD8, a gay restaurant in Kensington frequented by Rudolph Nureyev, I became a patron. I give this snapshot not to deepen the impression that I enjoyed a bisexual life with ballet dancers, but rather to show that I moved in exalted circles of wildly wilful, imaginative and creative people, and when I spoke to anyone about lifehouse socially, they were encouraging and enthused. Frank and I had been introduced by Kit Lambert who told me we would all three together develop the script I'd written. We never did, and for a while I wondered why. Recently Frank explained that behind my back Kit had confused him, saying my idea was unworkable, that Frank should go through the motions, then let it fade and move on to the more important project, a movie of *Tommy* which Kit hoped to direct as his first feature. Frank did not let the project drop. He arranged a regular weekly concert at the Young Vic, and held a press-conference during which I explained the general idea.

Tremendous confusion followed. I had planned to conduct rather simple experiments during these concerts producing pieces of music for some loyal audience members. I had no hope of producing anything like the expansive music I had envisioned and attempted to describe in my fiction, but certain people around me believed that was my target. Whispers of 'madness' fluttered backstage like moths eating at the very fabric of my project. In order to get The Who into the film, I figured I would make them look as though they were making the musical part of the experiment work: documentary film of our concerts would later be incorporated into the fiction of the film, so the concert (the one at which Bobby's audience disappears) would be a genuine one, not a lash-up by some power-crazed film director. The press conference was the beginning of the end. I was portrayed by some as confused when I was merely tired, and by some as arrogant when I was merely deeply committed to the idea that the story would work, that The Who could pull it off.

Within a few weeks our 'experiments' had dwindled into trips to the local pub and over-loud, short concerts of our early hits for anyone who showed up at the Young Vic. One of these unadvertised and thus poorly-attended concerts (of which I remember only two) was recorded and produced a reasonably good live tape. Eventually, exhausted and disillusioned, I abandoned the idea of making a film, and when Kit invited me to New York to start working on a straightforward recording at the Record Plant, a wonderful new studio there, I jumped at it.

When I got to New York I found that Kit had changed, and not entirely because he had become a heroin user. I realised later he had been deeply hurt by my failure to see how desperately he wanted to produce and direct a movie of *Tommy* and I had blocked him, fearing I would lose my mentor and friend to Hollywood. I lost him anyway. At the time, in New York, I was still obsessed with my own problems and was unaware of all this. He had completely lost all affection for me and began calling me not 'Pete', but 'Townshend', or 'Pete Townshend'. The recordings we made in New York were very good, but I left the druggy scene as soon as I could. The brilliant recording finally made by Glyn Johns was knocked off quickly in London when we all finally got back. It was entitled 'Who's Next', and the story of **lifehouse** wasn't even mentioned on the sleeve. Several songs vital to the plot were left off – 'Pure and Easy' being especially important.

After twenty years, I became obsessed with telling the story behind my failure to complete what was a genuinely good idea for the first genuine rock musical film. The obsession to do this was greater than the desire to complete the original film itself, and led to 'Psychoderelict', my last solo album of 1993.

Briefly, the story of *Psychoderelict* as it was performed by me in 1993

In *Psychoderelict*, Ray High, a reclusive rock star (not entirely dissimilar to the fellow parodied in *Private Eye*'s 'Celeb' cartoon strip), during a serious emotional crash, and from a place of extreme isolation, rediscovers an aborted project from his past, which brings him hope. The story is set in the world of rock-celebrity excess, but is actually about a different kind of self-abuse to that most commonly associated with that world. Ray High has cut himself off from every 'high'. He allows himself no fixes, there is no love in his life, no fans, no music, no present, no recovery nor rehabilitation, just a kind of apologetic tipsiness that allows him to survive petulantly, at a distance from his old friends and family. Only a few voices penetrate his existence. One is that of Rastus, an old road-manager who is trying to get Ray back on the road. Another is Ruth Streeting, an acerbic journalist, once a fan herself, but today more powerful than Ray. Another is Rosalind, a new fan of that uncertain age between childhood and the rest, who sends Ray a salacious photo and revives him from his gloom. I should quickly say that Ray High's experience does not entirely reflect my own. (Incidentally, the name Ray High was concocted as an amalgam of two rock contemporaries of whom I'm most fond, Ray Davies and Nick Lowe.)

Ray's forgotten project from the past is of course based on **lifehouse**. Ray is cajoled by Rastus, manipulated by Ruth Streeting and intoxicated by Rosalind (for whom he writes a hit song) and manages to get his version of **lifehouse** – called 'Gridlife' – on stage. It is a tremendous success, but he remains a little jaded, and yet nostalgic. I tried to deliver a double irony: Ray prefers to look back to a time when he was still able to look ahead. The play closes as he begins to forget his recent success, pores over new letters and pictures from new fans, and resentfully bemoans his great, lost hippy days of the seventies.

I wrote some quite beautiful songs for *Psychoderelict*, and as I listened to them on the finished CD, I realised I had been more deeply wounded by the failure of **lifehouse** than I had previously been able to admit. My problem was not simply one of failure to let go of the idea, or an unwillingness to accept defeat. I had been, in a sense, humiliated and broken by its non-appearance as a drama. It is, as you have read, quite simple. What was once seen to be incomprehensible was the background setting of the play: a world in which entertainment and global information and communication become dangerously intertwined. That idea is not hard for us to grasp today. In fact, in my first draft, I came up with my own version of 'Virtual Reality' as a device by which I could immerse the creatures of my story in total isolation, just as I had with the sensually-deprived Tommy. This neoteric idea is today framed by the more practical and elegant term 'couch-potato'.

In this playscript – the definitive version of l i f e h o u s e – Jeff Young, Kate Rowland and I decided not to try to further predict any problem with the current march of technology, and ignore common phobias about it. After all, in the current climate, to describe the future is to describe tomorrow, possibly even some daft science-fiction writer's yesterday. Here we speak not of 'grids', or the virtual reality 'experience suits' of my 1971 story, but of 'tele', 'hackers', 'pirates' and of course 'web-sites'. In his latest book Ray Kurzweil, who invented the repeatable, triggered digital recordings (called 'samples') so beloved of modern composers, predicts that within twenty years a wise and benign cyborg will be walking down Oxford Street with arms outspread entreating us all to 'follow him'. My future phobia in the 1971 l i f e h o u s e was that we might all become like spiritually perfect cyborgs, and perhaps be contented, but our hearts would be empty. We would owe it all to Rupert Murdoch (who was still in Australia in 1971 I think). In a time when rock concerts occasionally did 'catch fire', especially those by The Who, the real heroes of the 1971 l i f e h o u s e were the audience, the people who showed up at the Big Show. There was a real sense of danger there. Better to congregate, dance, worship and possibly die than to live in a bubble.

Here in the 1999 BBC script, the hero of the story – another Ray – is a rather simple man who remembers two voices from his childhood. One is his own childlike voice of around nine- or ten-years-old, imagining the future, delighting in the certainty that we would all one day blow ourselves to bits. The other is an imaginary friend from that childhood, a kind of Uncle-In-Overalls who replaces the emotionally-distant, war-ravaged father who can only recommend to the kid that he sits and quietly watches the newly-acquired miracle of a tiny, grey-screened telly. The Ray character landed firmly during creative sessions with Jeff Young and Kate Rowland. We suddenly realised we must accept that my phantom presence in the story was more forcefully felt than I had intended. I occasionally spoke in these creative meetings of the 'tragedy' of my time, and the 'moral cowardice' of my generation. There has been no great bomb since that last one dropped on Japan, but there has been a steady erosion of what is natural. As my art school mentor Gustav Metzger says, nature has been replaced by 'environment'. We no longer know the true values of natural life and art. We are slowly destroying ourselves in an 'autodestructive' society. My adolescent guitar smashing and early nihilistic lyrics returned during these latest **Lifehouse** discussions not to haunt or taunt but to remind me that thirty years ago with my contemporaries I had a chance to build and contribute to a better world. Had I done that? Tragically, I realised I had not. I had merely been a skilful and loquacious pop-artist.

My contact with my audience has always been unconscious, but ultimately processed and analysed. I've always known where I've just come from, placing great emphasis on understanding the journey itself, rarely planning properly where I would end up next. It is a childlike way to work, well suited to the life of a writer of pop songs. Not so useful for books. I remembered that, when I gathered my collection of prose writing, *Horse's Neck*, my editor Robert McCrum urged me to accept that my readers would always come to my writing believing they knew me inside out, and that if I pretended to be able to deceive them with my fictions, I would fail. He was right. Thus it was that fiction mixed with or perfumed by experience became 'autobiographical prose', even though many of the stereotypical rock 'n' roll events that I described had never happened. With Robert's good advice in mind, and extrapolated into lifehouse, we decided that we must let 'little Pete' speak. When we did, we found a captivating fellow full of suburban, bomb-site spunk and really bright ideas. We called him Rayboy, and he was most brilliantly recreated for me by Jeff Young who recorded my childhood memories very carefully.

Rayboy was, however, something of a pessimist. In our play the adult Ray grows up failing to realise his dreams and visions. I have, of course, realised many of my own childhood dreams, and I feel today that the few that are unrealised are within my grasp, or within my scope. But Ray and Rayboy are still very much of me. Perhaps they are also of my audience and childhood friends: all those West Londoners and Carnaby Street immigrants from Ireland or the Caribbean who some-times turned to me and said that I had a knack of putting into words what they could party-dance away, but found hard to otherwise express. It turned out that what I was best at putting into words for them was the frustration that they could not put anything into words.

What is probably important to say now is that when you hear this play on the radio, the music will not change your understanding of the story. That was never my intention. Much of the music featured in the play is used by Kate Rowland in an almost incidental way, but I hope in a manner that could not be improved upon. She is especially good at using music in drama. But what the many *descriptions* of 'music' in the play offer are gentle realisations of some of the New Age Millennial notions argued by the play's protagonists.

These may appear to be rather cosmic ideas, but I implicitly believe in them. In **lifehouse**, music itself is a fundamental and rudimentary principle, almost a functional character. To a musician like me, music is what is 'inside us all'. It represents experience, emotion and spiritual potential. I have invested my leading characters with this belief.

To go even further, I have always hoped that the **lifehouse** concert referred to in this play can happen in reality. I imagine a celebratory gathering at which a large number of individuals hear modest compositions or songs created specifically for them. In a finale, all those pieces could be combined, perhaps with creative and engaging images of each subject. I believe the result would have enormous impact and significance. I recently wrote a proposal to a friend of mine who owns a computer company (that for now I shall call Threshold), that is going to sponsor events of this kind:

Threshold to the lifehouse
From vision to reality.

In 1971, as the follow-up to his hugely successful rock-opera *Tommy*, Pete Townshend wrote **lifehouse** for The Who. **lifehouse** was first drafted by Pete Townshend as a film script. The film project stalled, but the legendary rock album 'Who's Next', was acclaimed by many as The Who's finest. Songs like *'Won't Get Fooled Again'*, *'Behind Blue Eyes'* and *'Baba O'Riley'*, have become part of the vertebrae of rock radio. A subsequent re-write brought forth '*Who Are You*' and '*Join Together*'. This year, 5 December 1999, the definitive story behind the famous songs was finally told when the BBC broadcast a radio play in the United Kingdom as part of their Millennium Drama series.

In the first draft of the play was a fictional scene that, at the time, seemed almost inconceivable in reality. In the finale of the film, members of an audience attending a concert provided personal data to composers working with powerful computers, and heard the results. Every single piece of music was then combined, and a mathematical – yet wonderfully creative – metaphor for the universality of the human spirit was demonstrated.

Thirty years on, as the Millennium dawns, Threshold Computers, in association with Pete Townshend, are going to make this fictional scene happen. *Threshold to the* Lifehouse will give everyone a chance to hear a piece of music specifically composed for them by Pete and his team. Indeed, their piece of music will be unique and special, produced using special computer programmes, based on data produced from a questionnaire accessed on the web, and perhaps even from DNA extracted from a hair of each participant. Pete will, in some cases, involve himself more deeply with participants, and develop lyrics or poetry to complement certain pieces of music.

On a date (yet to be set) in the future, an event will be held at which many of the pieces of music will be heard in public for the first time. Impudently, there will also be an attempt to realise Pete's 1971 vision for The Who's 'lost' movie project, and every single piece produced in the exercise will be combined and broadcast world-wide. We could hear the Music of the Spheres, or a busy night on Broadway. Pete believes we will hear the ocean.

Threshold Computers make buying and working with computers easier for people. Now they are making it easier for people to step into their own creative reflection.

Threshold to the lifehouse.

But this is perhaps just my composer's megalomaniacal dream. Such visions must be realised rather than described. That much I have learned on my lifehouse journey, which ends here. Thus I move quickly onto the reality. By the time you read this I will have released a CD package containing all the music inspired by the lifehouse story over the last twenty-nine years. This package will be called 'The lifehouse Chronicles'. A limited edition of 2001 will be called 'The lifehouse Method' and each will contain a unique code and a free ticket to the as yet unscheduled lifehouse Concert. Both packages will be available from my commercial web-site: www.eelpie.com. This is an excerpt from the brief I am giving to my software designers.

Brief for the Method

○ The 'Method' package will offer access to music generation software.

○ Each 'Method' package will contain a signed certificate from me with a unique code.

○ This code will unlock a deeper area of software.

○ The software should be available in all computer formats and can be distributed and 'shared', used without the code.

○ The code, when entered, will bring up a special data-entry page which will lead the user through a process that produces a one-off, unique piece of music, that contains a unique lyric generated by lyric motifs written by me.

○ Users of the 'Method' can take their completed unique composition to the Pete Townshend web-site, and expect to have their music developed further as the software is deepened. This process might unfold over a period of months or years.

○ The end-aim is that many buyers of the 'Method' will attend a concert in future at which their piece of music is 'premiered' and contrapuntally or fractally combined with other pieces.

○ Attendance at this concert is guaranteed and free to every purchaser of the 'Method' package whether they take part in the experiment or not.

So, I still have this crazy urge to make the fiction real. Sadly, this particular package will not be cheap. It contains four hours of music – the entire play as broadcast by the BBC – and is lavishly packaged. It also contains that guaranteed concert ticket and my promise that the buyer will be treated there like a V.I.P. But if you don't wish to come to my **lifehouse** party, or enjoy the fine art of 'The Method', you can buy the cheaper 'Chronicles'. You can enjoy the story, the story behind the story, and wait for the next chapter, which I hope will be some down-to-earth concerts, possibly a Broadway musical (most likely based on *Psychoderelict*) and perhaps a feature film. Of course my next chapter should really be an air-conditioned motor-caravan on its way South, but I am enjoying my work too much at present to take a holiday.

What is the story for? Why should it be heard? This play is essentially about the necessity for human beings to congregate regularly in order to share their emotions, and their responses to the spiritual challenges of art, great and small. This is something we are especially conscious of in this Millennium year. Even the British Government are putting on a show that could have been some seventies rock star's idea of a good night out. In this play, as a writer of fiction, and the bearer of post-apocalyptic wounds and generational shame, I suggest that the party might not end quite as they hope. Less seriously, I predict most of us will merely get drunk and laugh a lot, just like any other December 31.

In any case, l i f e h o u s e was never meant to be about 'prediction'. Since David Lister (the *Independent*'s art editor) gave me the front page recently, quoting the head of BBC Radio Drama (who also just happened to be directing the play) as saying that I'd foreseen the Internet thirty years ago, I've had a certain amount of sarcasm directed at me. That's OK. But I really did know the next big deal in future media would be paid for by sex, or music. I wasn't the only one. 'Sex' and 'MP3' (music downloading software) are the big web-words these days, so it is said. Both words get used in billions of searches every year. But downloading sex is still bigger than downloading music. I use the internet, but real sex is better than virtual sex, listening to music is better than talking about it, buying it on CD is better than waiting six hours while it downloads and then doesn't play properly because your computer is two weeks too old. Music you can hold is so marvellous: shiny CDs, slick black vinyl, wobbly cassettes and fiddly Minidisks – I love them all. They are the living flesh of the pop music industry.

I still like to make the odd prediction. Watching a sci-fi film recently I wondered what it is that makes their directors feel that all space ships will look *rusty* in the future. I wondered what spaceships would really be made of, and what they would look like. Plastic? Shiny metal? Something self-repairing, like flesh? I believe that in the future, all machines will be made of *flesh*. And for good measure, they will sigh, swoon and sing when polished. In twenty years a beautiful cyborg with a body of genuine flesh will walk down Oxford Street with her arms outstretched saying, '. . . come to The Lifehouse, your song is here.'

October 8th 1999

scene one

Rayboy   [Sings]   One Note, sounds like a light ray,
              One Note, sounds like a new day,
              One Note, holds all the others,
              Millions of colours,
              So One Note is best!

**Night time in a faraway place – a kind of North –
somewhere beyond the kind of place we know. We can
hear that it is night time and we can hear the wind
breathing. It is a weather that speaks, and there are two
words that it whispers, twisting garlands of words, and
they are . . .**

. . . life

house

life

house . . .

. . . life

house

life

house . . .

21

We hear the opening notes of *'Baba O'Riley'* through which the voices of Ray and Rayboy overlap and interweave.

Ray   When I was a boy I designed the future. It wasn't like the picture in my comic full of rockets and a city on the moon. It wasn't going to be like that. The future was a great big empty place where everyone was watching . . .

Rayboy   . . . and everyone was listening to a man, and he was telling them what to do and what to buy and what to *think* and even what to dream . . . My Dad was always laughing saying 'You playing with your crayons?' and I'd say I was colouring in a picture of tomorrow. 'Come and watch the programme', he'd say, pointing at the television flickering in the room. But I'd shake my head, say 'No', because I knew the *man* was in the telly. He was waiting 'til he had us hooked and then he'd wash our brains . . .

Ray   . . . and so I'd crayon in the future that the man was going to sell us, and the colour that I crayoned it was grey . . . so bloody grey . . .

'Baba O'Riley' [Orchestral, 1999] bleeds into . . .

scene two

Bleak northern wind fills the sky. Ray walks through the field and finds Sally, his wife.

Sally   I thought you were a scarecrow walking West.

Ray   I *feel* like a bloody scarecrow. What are you doing?

Sally   I'm sitting in a field.

Ray   How long have you been doing that?

Sally   About twelve years.

Ray   Still dark. What time is it?

Sally   Six. Christ; look at you.

Ray   What?

Sally   Been fighting?

Ray   Keep waking up.

Sally   Couldn't sleep at all. Saw this field out the

window, thought 'That's for me'. Came out here. Sat down. *Our* field.

Ray   I once dug up a spadeful of this soil and gave it to Mary in two cupped hands. 'This is gravity', I said. 'Everybody has their own supply. This is yours. One day it will run out. Then you'll join the wind'.

Sally   Have you ever climbed that mountain?

Ray   Once with Mary and all it was was a higher place than this. When you're up that mountain you quite fancy the valley.

Sally   Sometimes it pays to *look* at where we are. Just sitting here looking as night rolls over, the thing it meant comes back to you, and you think you can stay.

Ray   You know what I like best about this place?

Sally   You *hate* this place!

Ray   No . . . *No.*

Sally   Then what?

Ray   The weather. The weather is a radio. Sweet songs. Soul songs . . .

Sally   Cabaret . . .

Ray   Purcell . . . You remember beauty's purpose . . .

Sally   Purpose? Wasn't that why we came here?

Ray   I don't remember.

Sally   We came here because *you* had a vision. Another one. Of what we could do. What life could be. You'd had it . . .

Ray   With the city. With work.

Sally   I *followed* you.

Ray   Why?

Sally   Because I *believed* in you.

Ray   Then I was wrong.

Sally   You should have thought of that.

Ray   You stand out in your field of potatoes and you think: 'Potatoes are potatoes' and all the crap you left behind crawls after you. Been here a month and I built an aerial as tall as a steeple to catch a quiz show. Been here a year I was hooking soaps. Numb as bloody ever.

Sally We came here for Mary . . .

Ray I'll find her; bring her back.

Sally But there's nothing *here* for her. That's why she disappeared. She wanted freedom.

Ray You search for freedom. Think you found it; you haven't. You've exchanged one place you want to leave for another. *Everywhere's* the same.

Sally Maybe freedom is sitting on your arse in a field of dead potatoes.

Ray I'll leave you to it then. It's going to rain.

Sally How do you know?

Ray Because the radio is playing rain.

Sally Well then, I'll sit in mud. Want to sit with me?

Ray No.

He walks away back to the house.

Sally Well then, I'll sit in mud alone.

We hear '*Baba O'Riley*' again.

scene three

A storm breaks and soon Sally returns to the house.
Ray is sitting in front of the television zapping from
channel to channel. He is shouting at the screen.

Ray   You come into *my* front room and you say
          that? Bloody fools, the lot of you.

Sally   What are you doing?

Ray   Same as you. Sitting. In mud. Alone.

We hear television interference, static bursts, like a
rupture.

Sally   You're shouting at the telly.

Ray   No I'm not.

Sally   You're shouting at someone *in* it.

Ray   Yes . . .

Sally   How do you know who's in there?

Ray   Oh, they're in there alright.

Sally   You talk to them more than you talk to me.

Ray   I talk to you.

Sally   You talk in *code*.

Ray   It's hard since . . .

Sally   Say it.

Ray   It's *hard*.

Sally   Say, 'Since Mary *disappeared*'.

Ray   *It's hard*!

Further static and scrambled voices rupture the programme he's tuned in to. Then the voice of the Hacker comes in, soft and seductive against a background of sampled sounds and distortion. Bursts of Scarlatti and '*Who Are You*'.

Hacker   . . . *Breathe* . . . *breathe* . . . *breathe* . . . who *is* this voice breathing a breath of fresh air into couch potato land? What's *he* doing in our living rooms crashing our favourite show? People, I'm *collecting* . . . Collecting the music of your heart and soul . . . I want to hear your pulse beats and the blood pumping through your veins . . . Because the night is *coming* . . . All back to *my* place . . . *one* place . . . *one* music . . . When's it happening? You'll *know* about it 'cos you'll *be* there. And what's the big night *called?* It's called the Lifehouse . . . *Lifehouse* . . . *Lifehouse* . . . Hear me breathing . . . Here comes *the Lifehouse* . . . breathe . . . breathe . . . breathe . . .

The broadcast ends and breaks down into static, then background noise.

Ray It's like my childhood dream. A house full of music.

Sally I don't understand him. He gives me the creeps.

Ray He's not talking to you. He's talking to her.

Sally Who is he? The Pied Piper?

Ray *He's* dreaming the future now. She's gone to find it. I'm going to look for her. *You're* happy here.

Sally Happy? *Happy*!

Ray Oh, God . . .

Sally How can I be *happy* when *our* . . .

Ray I know . . .

Sally *Our daughter* . . .

Ray *I know.*

Sally Then *say it.*

Ray It depends what you mean by disappeared.

Sally I mean missing . . . maybe dead.

Ray No.

Sally We have to come to . . .

Ray No.

Sally . . . terms with the fact that she *might* be.

Ray I have to go. You'll be alright.

Sally I'll be *alone.*

Ray There are the neighbours.

Sally We don't know who the neighbours are. All
the people we're afraid of *followed* us here. Our
neighbours live down dirt tracks and come and

go in the night. Our neighbours are just shadows behind nets watching TV . . . *planning* things.

Ray   Planning what?

Sally   I don't know . . . Further disappearances?

Ray   You make it sound so dangerous here.

Sally   *Everywhere* is dangerous now.

Ray   Which is why I have to go. Someone has to do something.

Sally   You think that I don't care.

Ray   I meant the police. The *police* have given up. I *know* you care. Listen, when I come back . . .

Sally   Not now Ray. When you get back . . . *If* you get back, we'll talk about it then.

Static ruptures, then there is a hollow, overpowering silence.

Sally   Listen.

Ray   To what?

Sally   To the silence. *That's* what we came here for.
No traffic. No sirens. No helicopters hanging
in the sky.

Ray   There is no silence here. You can *hear* the
darkness.

Sally   Don't. You'll make me scared.

They listen. The world fills up with weather.

Ray   Hear it? The dark is where the music grows.
It's where the carnivals are.

Sally   Silence. Total silence . . . except . . .

Ray   Except what?

Sally   Dawn chorus. I can hear the birds. They're
singing out their greeting to the brand new day.

Ray   No . . . No, they're not.

Sally   Well, what are they singing then?

Ray   They're telling each other that they survived
the night.

'Behind Blue Eyes'[1971].

scene four

Ray is alone. The television is blasting. He kicks it to smithereens. Music cuts and breaks into *'Won't Get Fooled Again'* [1971].

scene five

We hear the sound of a vehicle engine spluttering to life. Song 'Won't Get Fooled Again' [1971].

Ray I wish I knew what to say.

Sally I wish . . .

Ray I have to go.

Sally You won't come back.

Ray I *have* to go.

Sally And I can't stop you.

Ray No.

Sally When people left the islands in the North they placed bibles open at Exodus in the embers of their fires.

Ray I haven't got a bible. If I left anything it would be the pictures I drew when I was a kid.

Sally Keep them with you. You might recognise
the world you used to know.

Ray Where the *fuck* did Mary go?

Sally She used up all her gravity. And then she flew
away.

Ray I don't know what to say.

Sally Phone.

Ray I will, I will; I'll phone.

Engine, music: '*Won't Get Fooled Again*' [1971].

scene six

The sound of the vehicle driving down the road. It is raining and the wipers mark time on the windscreen. These sounds shift into a different acoustic as the voice of Ray as a child speaks out.

Rayboy . . . These are my wax crayons that smell like candles on a cake. This is a house I made from blue and yellow. This squiggle is the path. I walk here. No one else does. My shadow is here. And my no-shadow. This is the Lifehouse. In the dark city . . . My house has noise inside its rooms and this noise is called music. I am drawing a face of a boy like me at the window. These squiggles in the sky that look like birds are lovely music.

Music comes into the child's world and then we move into Ray's world in the vehicle. Music fills his journey.

Ray I used to design this day in sketch books. The last day of the century . . . It was full of rain then and it's full of rain now . . . a child's rain . . . an old rain.

**We go back into his childhood world and the boy
speaks. The voices of Ray and Rayboy interweave.**

Rayboy These blue lines in the sky, they're not
rain*drops*; they're rain*lines*. They come down
into the picture and they stick into the roof of
the house . . . This is me inside the house, and
these are the zeds that say I'm sleeping . . .

Ray I used to get up in the morning and I
couldn't tell my Dad what the dreams were
about . . .

Rayboy . . . 'I heard the coloured music', I tried to tell
him . . .

Ray . . . and he'd say, 'We wasn't playing records,
son! It's too early in the day for party
dancing'.

Rayboy . . . And Dad says it's called fever. But it's
the noise called music, and it's lovely and it's
strange . . .

Ray . . . And because Dad wouldn't listen, or
because I couldn't *explain* . . . well, it was back
to waxy crayons and the house that I'd been
dreaming, and the bright splash of colour that
was all about the tune . . .

Rayboy . . . and this is me waking up . . . and all this

37

stuff coming out of my mouth like a rainbow
is a kind of coloured tra la la la la . . . !

**Ray gets out of the truck and walks through the
rain-lashed landscape. He starts to sing '*Bargain*'.
And the song takes over, flying far across the wilds.**

scene seven

As Ray spins round in his dervish dance another man approaches him. This is the Caretaker, a mythical figure from his past.

Caretaker   Hello ... still got that jam jar full of moths?

Ray   No. I let them go ... [Confused] What the *hell* are you doing here?

Caretaker   I just thought I'd see how you were getting on. It's been years. I thought you'd never turn up.

Ray   Turn up where?

Caretaker   In the Middle of Nowhere.

We hear the voice of Ray as a child.

Rayboy   This is a picture called The Middle of Nowhere ... This is a man who says 'Take care', and he's like a man in a comic. I made him up. At first I had him living in the trees, but there were no trees where we lived, so then I had him as a man in dark shadows after that and I made him up *so scary* that everyone was frightened of even the mention of his *name*.

And back to confused Ray in the Middle of Nowhere.

Ray I thought I'd seen the last of you.

Caretaker You never write, you never phone

Ray Because I don't *need* you any more.

Caretaker Why not?

Ray Because I'm a . . . a *man* for Christ's sake.

Caretaker [Sniggering] Ooh . . .

Ray What?

Caretaker Nothing. Just 'Oh'. There used to be a war, and that's when we were born. I *liked* the war. I like what it left behind, which is lots of holes where buildings used to be where you can sneak around and hide, and take short cuts to school . . . This is where I live, in dark places like that . . .

Ray Look . . . I don't need this. I'm in a big enough scrape.

Caretaker It was scrapes that we were good at. The Little Man and the Take Care bloke. I'm amazed we weren't locked up. It's no wonder your Dad didn't like me.

Ray He didn't *know* you.

Caretaker The drawings of me then. He didn't like the drawings.

Ray No.

Caretaker He used to screw them up.

Ray Yes . . . That was out of my hands. Dads call the shots when you're a . . .

Caretaker Little Man.

Ray Yes. When you're a . . . a kid. So how are you?

Caretaker Lonely.

Ray There's nothing I can do about that. I'm lonely too. I *need* to be alone. So when you're ready, if you'd just . . .

Caretaker Sorry for breathing. I'll be off then . . . And, oh yes . . . take care . . .

Ray Yeah, you too.

Caretaker Take care
    take care
        take care . . .
Take care
    take care
        take care . . .

He fades away.

Ray [Shouts] Where are you going? Don't leave me here . . . Christ!

He takes out his mobile phone and calls home.

Ray Come on Sally . . . Sal . . . Pick up . . . [Impatient] Pick up the phone!

She picks up.

Sally Hello?

Ray It's me.

Sally Where are you?

Ray I'm in the Middle of Nowhere . . . The strangest thing . . . A man came up to me, out of the darkness . . .

Sally Is this to do with Mary?

Ray No. Thing is Sal, I *recognised* him . . .

Sally From the photo-fits on the news?

Ray No . . .

Sally You *knew* him?

Ray Yes. I . . . I *invented* him.

Sally I see.

Ray When I was a kid.

Sally Yees . . .

Ray He used to live in dark shadows and the bombed out houses from the war.

Sally Oh, Christ. Have you been at the bottle?

Ray No . . . *Listen* to me.

Sally No. You listen to *me*. There's talk about all kinds of disappearances here. People are so thoughtless. I feel sick.

Ray Talk? Where?

Sally At Supermart.

Ray I thought we weren't shopping there again.

Sally It's the only place I can get the things I need.

Ray We *grow* what we need.

Sally What we grow's dead. Like Mary.

Ray She's *not* dead.

Sally She is if you listen to the gossip.

Ray I don't.

Sally You're listening all night. There's gossip all over the wires. People are disappearing all the time, Ray, never to be seen again.

Ray Where *are* you?

Sally I'm in the Supermart queue.

Ray You can't talk about things like that in a Supermart queue.

Sally Well don't phone me when I'm here then. Look . . . this is ridiculous.

Ray What are you buying?

Sally   *What?* Potatoes. I'm *buying* potatoes.

Ray   But we bloody *grow* potatoes.

Sally   We grow *dead* potatoes.

Ray   Listen Sal, I *need* to talk.

Sally   Come home Ray, and *then* I'll listen to you.

Ray   But I don't know where I am.

Sally   Look it up on the map.

The line cuts out and then goes dead.

Ray   Sally . . . Sal . . . I'm no good with bloody
         maps.

He redials. No answer. He puts the phone away.

There *are* no maps of Nowhere.

'*Baba O'Riley*' [1971].

scene eight

Back in the vehicle, Ray searches the airwaves for
music but is bombarded with adverts for catalogues and
washing up liquid, and conditioners for fabrics, carpets,
hair . . . then a voice comes through the jingles and
blows them all away. It is the voice of the Hacker in a
confiding whisper, to a background of Scarlatti.

Hacker   *Whisper . . . whisper . . . whisper* these words All
          this *shit* they're junk pumping you with . . .
          yeah *you* slobbing on the couch . . . You so full
          of junk can't even move, can't even think.
          Don't listen to *that* . . . listen to *this* then switch
          this machine *off* . . . Open the windows . . . let
          in the air and the wind . . . It's blowing over
          the wires like a voice in the *sky* . . . Blowing in
          from the *sea* . . . Hear it breathing? Hear all
          that war going on out there? *Sure* . . . ! But
          listen up close and hear the sound of children
          playing in the streets . . . blowing in from so
          long ago you've probably forgotten how it
          sounds . . . Instead of all this Day-Glo gloop
          that turns your dreams to nightmares . . . let
          me hear . . . Like a congregation . . . Having a
          conversation It's called *communication* . . . Whisper

46

it back in reply . . . It's coming fast . . . things are changing . . . It's the *Lifehouse* . . . whisper it . . . It's the *Lifehouse* . . .

scene nine

Ray turns the radio down and pulls over to the side of
the road. He switches off the engine. Occasional sounds
of a passing car on wet tarmac.

> Ray   This is the land that kid on the radio hates.
> Mary could be in a place like this . . . bundled
> up in a car boot by some Foto-Fit face . . .
> The rain washes the colour out and all that's
> left is grey . . .

And into . . .

> Rayboy   . . . And the future needs bright colours.

> Ray   I was going to grow up and save the world like
> some Superman from the back streets with
> Crayola instead of Kryptonite . . .

> Rayboy   Dad'd ask me what I'd been doing, and I'd say
> I was talking to a *man* about the future where
> I'm going to go one day . . .

> Ray   And he'd clip me round the ear and say I
> must not talk to strangers. Clip, clip, each ear

clipped . . . and with two ears hot and stinging we'd sit down and watch TV and get lost in its magical worlds . . .

Rayboy   And we'd sit close . . .

Ray   And I could feel his warmth . . . And the pain would disappear . . .

He shouts into the weather.

Oh Mary . . . *Mary*. Where the *fuck* is Mary?

And music fills the place up as if it is blowing up the motorway. We hear the song '*Who Are You*' [Gary Langan]. From the truck radio comes static and the voice of the Hacker calling people.

Hacker   . . . I'm still collecting your music, and *you're* still coming to the Lifehouse . . . You're coming from all over . . . You're coming to the Lifehouse . . . the *Lifehouse* . . . the *Lifehouse* . . . What music's he *talking* about . . . ? *Heart* music . . . *Soul* music . . . *Your* music . . . You're all out there . . . You're *all* coming together . . . And we're gonna hear the music that will change your *world* . . . At the *Lifehouse* . . .

scene ten

The Hacker is in his lair broadcasting from the top of a
city high-rise when Mary turns up.

Hacker   Lifehouse . . . Lifehouse . . . Who are you?

Mary   Mary. I'm a fan.

Hacker   I'm not a pop star. I don't *have* fans.

Mary   What I mean is . . . You're the Voice. I listen.

Hacker   [To listeners] I'll be back . . . back . . . ba . . .
[He switches off] You shouldn't have come
here.

Mary   I wanted to see you.

Hacker   If you can find me, *they* can find me.

Mary   Who are *they*?

Hacker   Who are *you*? Shit . . .

Mary   There's loads of Me's. It's the only thing
there is.

Hacker   What?

Mary   Your broadcasts.

Hacker   Transmissions.

Mary   Oh, *dead* technical.

She starts poking around.

Hacker   Excuse me? Look, I don't need this. I've got things to do.

Mary   Well I'm not going . . . I just want to sit and listen.

Hacker   But that's the point. I never know who's listening. You get this picture of your voice coming into people's houses and it's like a secret. Me talking to this person sharing the secret. I can tell them anything. They'll listen; they trust me; never heard a voice like mine. You get this picture of a listener all huddled and hidden. And then when one of them tracks you down, it's some kid who's a pop fan.

Mary   I'm not a pop fan. I'm here because you're the only thing there is.

Hacker Where do you listen?

Mary In the Back of Beyond. My Dad's got this
van full of machines. I sneak in at night and
twiddle through the stations. They're all the
same . . . and then *you* come in like a wild
one. You know those parties where aunties
drink sherry and babble on about nothing?
Well, you're the bad boyfriend who staggers
in bringing the world with him and pisses
everybody off.

Hacker Boyfriend?

Mary Scared stiff of me aren't you? Think I'm some
dumb groupie who's down here for a shag.

Hacker Wouldn't be the first time. How about it?

Mary You think I've come all this way just to . . .

Hacker Well, why *are* you here then?

Mary The world you talk about . . . It's not just me
that's coming here today. I want to be here
when it happens. It's gonna be . . .

Hacker Gonna be what?

Mary I don't know . . . Dangerous?

Hacker   [Broadcasts] If it's the last thing you do, at
least you know you're living . . . *At the Lifehouse*
. . . [He switches off].

Music comes back in : *'Who Are You'* [Live, 1999].

Mary   Beats sitting at home with Mum and Dad
and . . . *nothing*.

Hacker   Do they know where you are?

Mary   Don't even know where I am when I'm in the
same room.

scene eleven

Ray walks down a path towards a derelict building. He opens the door and goes in, scattering birds. He walks across broken glass and timber.

      Ray   The ruins of a man in the ruins of a church . . .

Even though he almost whispers this, it echoes through the ruin.

> I once had a jam jar crammed tight with a
> hundred moths. I let them go in church
> while all the women muttered prayers . . .
> The superstitious whispers said the moths
> were mouthing messages from heaven's dear
> departed . . . Some women clapped their
> prayer books shut and trapped them tight
> between communion and psalm . . . *All*
> churches are empty, but the ghost voices of
> long gone congregations are still moth-
> breathing their hymns . . .

We hear the faint murmur of a hymn blown by the wind. He climbs the staircase up to the belfry. A solemn dull thud echoes through the crumbling building as he rings

the broken bell. The bell subsides. He calls out, which
echoes. The Caretaker appears.

Ray   I don't know what to do.

Caretaker   Why don't you say a prayer?

Ray   And who would I be praying to?

Caretaker   There might be *someone* there.

Ray   Then what would I be praying *for*?

Caretaker   You could pray for your daughter.

Ray   She can't be found with a prayer.

Caretaker   Sing something then.

Ray   Why?

Caretaker   To make the place echo one more time before
it dies.

Ray   I wouldn't know what to sing.

Caretaker   There was a hymn you used to sing when you
were in the choir.

Ray   [Laughs] I used to sing the darkest hymns to
Mary. They were lullabies of gloom.

Caretaker   Then sing! And maybe you'll get a glimpse of
where she is.

Ray begins to sing.

Ray   And did those feet
In ancient times
Walk upon England's mountains . . .

**But cannot carry on. He climbs back down the bell
tower steps.**

Caretaker   [Disappointed] that could have been *really* nice.

Ray   [Irritated] What?

Caretaker   I thought you were going to *reclaim* it there for
a moment. Make it *ours* again.

Ray   Ours?

Caretaker   The *people's*.

Ray   It's just a bloody song I used to sing.

Caretaker   Well, I liked it.

Ray   Doesn't really matter *what* you like though,
does it?

56

Caretaker   You're *scared*.

Ray   Of what?

Caretaker   Of the *dark*. Alone in all the birdywing
black.

Ray   You're here.

Caretaker   Don't *have* to be. I can be off. Quick as spit.

Ray   *No*!

Caretaker   Need me?

Ray   No ... yeah ...

Caretaker   Then have some ... *respect*.

Ray   You're mad.

Caretaker   You *dumped* me. Where the hell do you think
I've been all these years waiting for *you* to be
scared again.

Ray   I'm *not* scared.

Caretaker   You fucking *will* be. Ta ta. [He vanishes].

Ray   *Wait*! [Which echoes through the church.
Then silence].

Somewhere in this church there'll be a bible
. . . open at Exodus.

He walks away and the ghost voices of the long-gone
congregation are heard on the wind. Music: *'Pure And
Easy'* [1971].

scene twelve

**Rapid cut to a different world, a different acoustic.
We are with Mary and the Hacker in his hideaway.**

Hacker   Where is he?

Mary   Far away in the Back of Beyond.

Hacker   He'll be worried.

Mary   Are you on his side?

Hacker   Not my business. Parents worry. Not that I
care. He might *miss* you? Like I'm bothered.

Mary   If he's noticed.

Hacker   What does he do?

Mary   Builds a house. And cries.

Hacker   About what?

Mary   Went out to the country to grow potatoes.
Can't grow them. He's crap.

Hacker Does he know where you are?

Mary No . . . Don't want him to.

Hacker You're one of those disappeared kids.

Mary I'm hardly a kid.

Hacker Did you make the papers?

Mary Don't know . . . been travelling.

Hacker Then you'll have been 'Spotted in Various Locations'. You'll get your own website if you disappear for long enough. Why did you run?

Mary To look for you. You're this voice. I listen all the night to all the voices – *your* voice most – I just listen. It's like adventures listening to you. And mysteries too. That's the other thing. Adventures and mysteries . . .

Hacker When did you run away?

Mary Weeks ago.

Hacker Then you're forgotten. They'll be onto someone else by now.

Mary And Mum'll think I'm dead, and Dad'll not have noticed.

Hacker   So you like them then?

Mary   What?

Hacker   Adventures and mysteries.

Mary   Yeah . . .

Hacker   Well, you *are* one.

Mary   I'm a mystery *and* an adventure! And I'll tell you who *you* are.

Hacker   Who?

Mary   *You're* The Voice.

He slams a Lifehouse 'jingle' into the deck. We hear it.

Hacker   . . . Wide awake still dreaming . . . of a better world than this . . . Looking for clues? Look to the bridges . . . Over your head . . . *Lifehouse* is the *only* place to be on this night . . . on the *Big Night* . . . Come to the Lifehouse . . . the *Lifehouse* . . .

scene thirteen

**Ray dials home on his mobile. The recorded message
kicks in after a few rings.**

> **Sally** You're through to Sally, Ray and Mary. There's
> **(voice)** no one here right now . . .

And then she picks up.

> **Ray** It's me . . . I thought *you'd* disappeared.

> **Sally** I was in Mary's room. Looking through her
> things. I thought I might find something. Like
> a clue.

> **Ray** And did you?

> **Sally** I found a tape, full of poems.

> **Ray** About what?

> **Sally** About the things she never talked to us about.
> Like *everything*. Like little slivers of *her*.

We hear Mary's voice on tape.

Mary   Open window / Big sky, night
Sneak through / black empty space
If I was a bird girl / I'd fly
Wild west wind / far from this place
Up above dark clouds / fly free
Dream fly high / sky's sweet bliss
Open window / set me free
Fly away! Fly away! / Far from *this* . . .

Ray   [Splutters] I didn't even know . . .

Sally   Perhaps we never know our children.

Ray   I thought . . .

Sally   You thought she was all junk, and training
shoes . . . and *kung-fu* games . . . and telly.

Ray   Yes.

Sally   She stopped being your little girl a *long* time
ago . . .

Ray   I don't understand why you've given up.

Sally   I don't *want* to give up; I feel *safer* giving up.
It's like putting the Given Up coat on. Then
later, if it *is* bad news . . . If she is . . .

Ray   She isn't.

Sally If she *is* . . . dead, then I'm already wrapped up against the cold.

Ray You miss her?

Sally I don't know *how* to miss her. I've hidden 'miss' away.

Ray There must be something at the end of all this.

Sally Maybe you'll find the 'something' . . . There's nothing I can say.

Ray It's all in your voice.

Sally What is?

Ray Blame.

Sally I keep wanting to say to you, 'If you hadn't done this . . . If you hadn't done that . . .'

Ray Then *say* it.

Sally I can't say it . . . I've said it . . . For Christ's sake, Ray, if you hadn't done a thousand things . . . Oh, forget it. Just forget it . . . Where *are* you?

Ray Up against the coast; going to take a look around.

Sally Don't stop phoning. I don't want you to . . .
And I want you to.

Ray Soon . . . I'll phone again soon.

He hangs up and drives on. He sees someone on the road ahead. He pulls over. Turns off the radio.

Ray Want a lift? . . . Climb in then . . .

And it's himself when he was a boy.

What are you doing in the Middle of Nowhere?

Rayboy I'm looking for someone.

Ray Do your parents know where you are?

Rayboy No . . .

Ray Well, they should do. It's dangerous.

Rayboy I'll do what I want and you can't stop me.

Ray I gave you a lift, so less of the cheek.

Rayboy This truck . . . *smells.*

Ray I didn't *have* to stop.

Rayboy   If you make me get out you'll only end up
                worrying.

Ray   Then try and be *nice*.

Rayboy   It smells of old men.

Ray   *Out*!

Rayboy   But it's *dangerous* out there.

Ray   Then try and be . . . *nice* . . . A runaway.
             Another bloody runaway. I was always running
             away when I was your age. I never *stopped*
             running away, come to think of it. I always ran
             away 'cos no one listened.

Rayboy   No one ever listens. I always say I'll run away
                to Timbuctoo or the long road to Tipperary.
                I go inside old houses and talk to dead men
                from the war. I make people up.

Ray   I used to make people up: still do. There's this
             man that used to take care of me.

Rayboy   A man who says 'Take care'?

Ray   Yes!

Rayboy   I chase the man down back cracks. *Flit*!
                Flit! he goes, through shadows. He's there,

and then he isn't there, like spit on the coals.

Ray   And his voice echoes, 'Take care, take care' . . .

Rayboy   And we talk about the future and where I'm going and about when *I'm* a man. I say, 'I'm going to the future', and he always says, 'Maybe I'll see you there' . . . !

Ray   You must never talk to strangers.

Rayboy   I'm talking to you.

Ray   I suppose you are. But then we don't quite *feel* like strangers.

Rayboy   You're . . . old.

Ray   Yes . . .

Rayboy   You're not what I expected.

Ray   [Deflated] Oh . . .

Rayboy   I thought you'd be . . . magnificent.

Ray   And I'm not?

Rayboy   No. You're all broken. All veins and a bobbly nose.

67

Ray   I'm no spring chicken, granted.

Rayboy   You should look after yourself more.

Ray   Yeah . . . well, look . . . where are you headed?

Rayboy   Don't know. Is that the sky or is it the sea?

Ray   It's the sea.

Rayboy   Right then. I think I'm heading there.

scene fourteen

Orchestral music – Purcell. The sound of a sluggish sea and of the vehicle pulling up on the sands. The engine is switched off and they get out. They walk towards the water. Musical echoes of a lost seaside past.

Rayboy   This is a brilliant place.

Ray   The proper bucket and spade place.

Rayboy   We came here on our holidays.

Ray   We used to too. Sandcastles with flags
and rubber rings just slightly going down;
dandelion and burdock coming out your nose.

Rayboy   [Laughing] The weather speaks words, doesn't
it?

Ray   Yes, I did know that, yes.

Rayboy   Listen.

They listen. The wind comes howling in and says . . .

Dad . . . Drop more pop, son . . . ?
You've caught the sun, son . . .
Rub a bit of cream in . . .
Wafer or a cornet . . . ?
Blow your rubber ring up . . .
Fancy the helter skelter . . . ?
Pass your Dad a kunzel cake . . .
Next year I fancy Brighton . . .

And the voice fades.

Rayboy That was like my Dad's voice . . .

Ray Memories blow towards us . . .

And then the sky is cut in two by the scream of fighter planes seemingly inches above their heads.

Rayboy [Shouting] What's that?

Ray It's called 'manoeuvres'.

Rayboy Are they going to a war?

Ray Yes.

Rayboy Which war?

Ray The last war of the century. When I was . . .

Rayboy   When you were little?

Ray   Yes. It was so peaceful then.

Rayboy   It was beautiful?

Ray   Yes. There used to be a fairground here in summer. The waltzers and the dodgems, where you got to dream that you might kiss a girl. Such beauty in such darkness.

Rayboy   I went there!

Ray   When?

Rayboy   Last year.

Ray   What year was that?

Rayboy   1954. The year after the Queen was in the telly.

Ray   I don't think I need to hear this . . . What year is it now?

Rayboy   Don't know.

Ray   It's the last day of the century. Tomorrow's zero zero.

Rayboy   Then it's the future?

Ray Yes. And look at it. Manoeuvres in the sky, black water from the oil spill . . .

Rayboy . . . 21 . . . 22 . . . 23 . . . 24 . . . 25 . . . 26 . . .

Ray What are you counting?

Rayboy Dead birds. I could guess a hundred. Like they're glued on the black water.

Ray Doesn't look like the sea. Looks more like rolls of lino.

Rayboy The waves come in and then go out. First there's the sea, and then there's the no-sea.

Ray Yes! The *no*-sea! The sea comes in, all dead birds and black gloop.

Rayboy And then the sea goes out and leaves the *no-sea* left behind. What's that funny boat thing floating out there near the sky?

Ray It's a television set! There's probably a man in an armchair too, watching adverts as he sinks beneath the waves.

Rayboy And he'll be down there forever . . .

Ray . . . thinking about what cat meat he should choose.

Rayboy This bird is pretty.

Ray What sort of bird is it?

Rayboy A *dead* bird.

Ray If you took that dead bird's voicebox, you could blow through it.

Rayboy Toot toot! The dead bird's song. In the future there are two fast jets doing a thing they call manoeuvres in the Middle of Nowhere sky. First there is the *no*-noise, then there is the *noise* going all along the black sea where the dead birds roll . . . This is the winter . . .

Ray It's nearly the end of the year . . .

Rayboy And all the birds are dead, and there's no songs . . .

scene fifteen

Mary and the **Hacker** are up on the rooftop with the city screaming, whispering, blaring down below. We hear the introduction of *'Join Together'* looped under the dialogue.

    Mary   [Shouting in the wind] It's amazing up here.

Hacker   Don't go near the edge! I don't want my groupie splattered all over the pavement.

    Mary   I'm *not* your groupie.

Hacker   Then why are you here?

    Mary   I just wanted to meet you. You come into the gloom and lights go on. Go *pop*! There's no one like you where I live . . . *used* to live . . .

Hacker   Oh there is . . . There's kids all over got the stuff to speak. Kids in tower blocks, kids on the move. You just hack into the grid and speak. It's a buzz. You feel your heartbeat speeding up and all the stuff comes out of you and you're telling stuff to kids like you who are listening in the dark.

74

Mary   The buzz. Is that why you do it?

Hacker   There are so many things to piss you off, you've got to speak to *someone*. They think this world's sewn up, but you can rip the seams a bit and slither through. You just blow in like the wind and scatter a seed here and there. Some nights, it feels like you're speaking to no one. Some nights it's like you're speaking to the whole world . . . And every single person at the Lifehouse will be listening to what I have to say.

Mary   You reckon you're It, don't you?

Hacker   Yeah . . .

Mary   I reckon you're It too.

scene sixteen

Ray and the boy are driving. Ray dials home on his mobile. Song: '*Join Together*'.

Ray   Pick up the phone . . . pick the – where the hell is she?

He slams the phone on the dashboard.

Rayboy   Where the hell are *we*?

Ray   [Still angry] I'm driving down the map. I'm looking for someone . . . looking around. I haven't looked for a long time and everything has changed.

Rayboy   Are they all funny places you look at? Like dead bird seas and motorways?

Ray   [Snappy] Yes.

Rayboy   And that. Is that Stonehenge?

Ray   [Calmer] Those are cooling towers.

Rayboy   They're beautiful.

Ray   The dark satanic mills.

Rayboy   That's like the lullaby . . .

Ray   . . . I sang to my daughter.

Rayboy   Have *you* got a daughter?

Ray   Yes. I *hope* I've got one. She writes *poems*.

Rayboy   Hope?

Ray   She's . . . disappeared.

Rayboy   You should have been a better dad, then maybe she'd have stayed.

Ray   Well, it's easy to get it wrong.

Rayboy   Do you tell her stories?

Ray   Used to . . . Not any more. I miss all that.

Rayboy   My Dad's always too busy.

Ray   Doing what?

Rayboy   Important things to do with his pipe. He needs us all to be quiet while all that happens.

Ray   I used to think that *he* was the dark satanic mill.

Rayboy   The *world* is full of smoke.

Ray   It's like graffiti on the sky.

Rayboy   Is this *really* the future?

Ray   Yes, I suppose it is . . . I suppose it is. Why?

Rayboy   I always draw the future.

Ray   With waxy crayons.

Rayboy   Yes.

Ray   See that bundle of paper in the back? They're pictures I made when I was a kid.

Rayboy   [Rummaging through papers] They're the same as mine.

Ray   I thought they might be . . . Do you like music?

Rayboy   Yes.

Ray   Then push that button there . . . let's play it loud . . .

We hear the song '*Going Mobile*'.

scene seventeen

The voice of the Hacker cuts through the song.

Hacker ... *Speak* ... *speak* ... *speak* to me ... let me
hear about the things that make you tick ...
All you people coming to the Lifehouse ...
I can *hear* you coming ... all your voices ...
heartbeats ... chords ... discords ... high
pulse ... low-sharp-fast-soft-slow ... *spirit*! ...
Everyone's coming to the *Lifehouse* ...

Mary He'll be listening to that.

Hacker Who?

Mary Dad. Listening and agreeing about your 'speak,
speak, speak,' but doing nothing about it.
Sitting in his van. Whistling. Like an old man
in a shed. Old men sit in sheds and whistle.
When they're not whistling they mutter.

Hacker About what?

Mary About *you* most probably. Old men like my
Dad *made* the world you're on about. He
needs ...

79

Hacker [He broadcasts] All you people who've been sending me their heartbeats . . . Everybody's music's gonna fit together on the *biggest . . . sweetest* night of the year . . . And we will make *one note* . . . And no-one's gonna stop us . . . If you want to *hear* that music . . . If you want to *make that music* . . . Then come to the *Lifehouse* . . . the *Lifehouse* . . . the . . . [He switches off] Needs?

Mary *Needs* a good talking to.

Hacker You *could.*

Mary Could what?

Hacker *Talk* to him.

Mary He wouldn't listen.

Hacker Who *does* he listen to?

Mary Pirates.

Hacker Exactly.

Mary What?

Hacker Be a pirate. Speak to the world. [He broadcasts] . . . *Speak* . . . *speak* . . . *speak* to me . . . let me hear about the things that make you tick . . .

All you people coming to the Lifehouse . . .
I can *hear* you coming . . . all your voices . . .
heartbeats . . . chords . . . discords . . . high
pulse . . . low-sharp-fast-soft-slow . . . *Spirit*! . . .
Everyone's coming to the *Lifehouse* . . .

Switch to the song '*Going Mobile*'.

scene eighteen

Ray and Rayboy are in the truck driving.

Rayboy   Sometimes I draw this picture where the
world is all wires going inside people's houses
and even inside their heads. People buy their
dreams . . . They're like tape recordings for
plugging in your sleep . . . I like dreams . . .
There's more to do there . . . Do you like
dreams?

Ray   [With a shudder] Not so much these days,
no . . .

Rayboy   You can be a cartoon and kiss Snow White
and you can be dead clever and a laugh . . .
And in the end you can be all jumbled up bad
and good and end up in the middle . . . The
man who sells the dreams mucks about with
them . . . He won't let people dream what they
want to dream . . . It's like he owns the wide
awake and now he wants to own the fast
asleep . . .

Ray   Your pictures all came true. The world *is* like
that now . . . Look at it . . .

Rayboy   Look at that writing on the bridge . . .

   Ray   I missed it. what did it say?

Rayboy   It said . . . L . . . I . . . F . . . E . . .

   Ray   Lifehouse . . .

Rayboy   Sometimes I draw a . . .

   Ray   Don't start on about the house again.

Rayboy   You're all bad tempered.

   Ray   I'm *trying* to drive. Can't listen to you wittering
            on *and* drive *and* look at bridges.

Rayboy   I only wanted to tell you about the picture.

   Ray   Well tough. Shit happens.

Rayboy   You said 'shit'.

   Ray   Christ! Sorry . . . Go on then . . . about the
            bloody house.

Rayboy   And all the world is locked away inside their
            little houses. And all the world is dreaming
            dreams that they've bought off the man who
            owns the world . . .

83

scene nineteen

Rayboy Where are you going now?

Ray Shut up, I'm phoning someone.

Ray telephones home. Sally picks up.

    Any news?

Sally She's just another one of the missing. There are *so* many children missing. Some are gone forever. The police were here. They say there's not much hope.

Ray There's always hope.

Sally Ah, the man who pretends he still possesses hope.

Ray You think I have no hope?

Sally You're bleaker than the land we came to live in.

Ray I'm *trying*.

Sally But what are you *doing*?

84

Ray   Don't know . . . talking to myself, mostly. Talking to people I meet. Going to places where people *used* to go but no one goes any more. You know . . .

Sally   You might as well come home.

Ray   No!

Sally   For all the good . . .

Ray   No. I'm going . . . I know where I'm going. I'm going back to the city.

Sally   Why?

Ray   Because that's where this whole thing started, and if I don't move I feel so bloody useless.

Sally   But what is it that you're *doing*?

Ray   I'm doing my best. That's what I'm doing. I'm *doing my best*.

Sally   I've seen fathers like you on the telly.

Ray   What?

Sally   Crying at press conferences.

Ray   Oh, don't do this to me.

85

Sally Pleading and weeping for the return of their *darling* little girl. They weep and wail. They hold their wife's hand. They gaze into the camera, into the living rooms of the land where all the other frightened parents sit in tears . . .

Ray What are you getting at?

Sally They always turn out to have done it. The crying father has *always* killed his daughter.

Ray *What*?

Sally I'm just telling you what I've seen on the telly.

Ray I *know* what's on the telly. I've *seen* the bloody telly. You think I don't *know* what's on the telly? I used to *work* for the *bloody telly*!

Sally I'm not saying that . . .

Ray Christ Almighty, I would *never* . . .

Sally No, I know. I'm not saying. Oh, shit. I don't *know* what I'm saying.

Ray I think you've said enough. Implying that I *might* do it makes me feel like I *did* do it. You're trying to drive me mad.

Sally You might already *be* mad.

Ray I'm your . . . I'm . . . *Ray.*

Sally I don't know *who* you are. You're not the Ray I remember marrying.

Ray Oh, Christ, I feel *so* sick.

Sally And so?

Ray And so I'm going.

Sally Leaving me?

Ray No! Going. Going now. I need to think . . . I'll phone you later. I just need . . .

Sally I might not be here.

Ray When I phone?

Sally When you come back.

Ray I'm *asking* you to be. We'll start again.

Sally There might not be enough that's worth a new beginning.

Song: '*Love Ain't For Keeping*'.

scene twenty

Service station. We hear snatches of conversation.

    Voices [Looped and interweaving throughout]
Turnoff at junction twenty-three / Apologise
for any inconvenience / Turn left . . . or is it
right at Nantwich / Win a free holiday at the
service station of your choice / Welcome to
Moto-Munch / They do a lovely all day
breakfast / I'm in the services . . . running
twenty minutes late / I want to see that plate
clean / Are we nearly there?

    Rayboy I'm frightened.

    Ray So am I . . . But I'm *hungry*.

    Rayboy All those shiny cars.

    Ray It's like they've come here for a party. The
Service Station New Year's Ball. Come on.

**They get out of the vehicle and enter the service
station. The main thing we hear is the sound of arcade
machines bubbling, distorted voices. They move**

through this world in awe. Music on the tannoy: '*Won't Get Fooled Again*' [1971].

Ray   So *this* is where all the people are.

Rayboy   Where are we?

Ray   Perhaps the heart of darkness . . . ? It's a Moto-Munch. These people probably *live* here . . . [He spots the **Caretaker**] Oh shit . . . Don't look. Keep walking.

Rayboy   Who are we hiding from?

Ray   No one. Just . . . don't . . . look.

The Caretaker presents himself.

Caretaker   Got the munchies?

Ray   Look. I don't *need* this. My life's in pieces and you're not helping.

Caretaker   Get yourself a cup of something, *then* you'll feel better. You're a bit stressed. I'll take care of things.

Ray   Stop saying that.

Caretaker   What?

Ray Take care.

Caretaker You used to like it . . . When you were a *little* man.

Ray Yes. But *now* I'm a *big* man.

Caretaker You sit down. I'll get a tray. Does the lad want change for the machines?

Ray *No!*

Caretaker Ooh! Calm down. Now, what do you want? The Chicken Chunks or the Burgo-Bap?

Ray I don't want any of that crap.

Caretaker I'll get you the Chuck Burger. It's a *yum!*

Ray I grow my *own* food.

Caretaker Not here you don't. Now pipe down. You're upsetting everyone.

Ray This place is *Hell.*

Caretaker You're overtired. Out of your depth.

Ray What the fuck's *wrong* with you? With *everyone?*

Caretaker They're excited. It's a big day.

Ray   They don't *look* excited.

Caretaker   People come here after Christmas for the balloons and paper hats.

Ray   The balloons are going flat.

Caretaker   Look at that waitress with the tinsel halo. *She's* having a laugh.

Ray   She's on the verge of tears. So am I.

Caretaker   You'll want a fizzy drink.

Ray   No I won't.

Caretaker   Will the lad want one? Want a fizzy pop?

Ray   He doesn't *want* a fizzy pop. You're *totally* immersed in crap.

Caretaker   *You* need a good night's sleep.

Ray   I want you to go away and leave me alone.

Caretaker   But I'm here for you.

Ray   Well I don't want you! Go *away*!

Ray starts to sob.

Caretaker   You're crying.

Ray   Yes. [To **Rayboy**] *You* deal with him.

Rayboy   Who?

Ray   [Livid] Oh, don't give me that. He was *your* idea. Sort it bloody out.

Caretaker   Well, you turned out to be a right bloody misery

And Ray starts throwing crockery and kicking out.

Caretaker   The security cameras are watching everybody, and everybody is watching you, so you either *sit down* or get out of here sharpish.

Ray   [Storming off] I just want something to eat. Excuse me, where can I get a . . . Hello-o?

The sound of televisions fills the world. They start running through the service station, through the madness of the game machine 'music', and then they are outside and there is silence except for the whirr of a single surveillance camera. Ray taps on the glass.

Ray   Hello . . . You inside the camera? Where can

we get a fucking cup of something? Where can we . . . hello?

Caretaker   They can see you. Get a grip!

Ray   I demand to see the manager. I . . .

And then in the shadows there is a huge almighty scuffle as Ray is kicked to pieces by unseen men. The sound of violence and Ray's groans echoing round the bins. Rayboy is terrified and screaming.

Rayboy   Leave him alone . . . *leave him.*

Until Ray emerges staggering into the light.

Ray   You stupid . . . What did you do *that* for?

Caretaker   Now we're evens.

Ray   For what?

Caretaker   For *dumping* me. When a friend's no longer needed what happens to him?

Ray   I don't know.

Caretaker   He gets *dumped. Fucking* dumped.

Ray   I think my nose is broken.

Caretaker   [Grabbing him] You're lucky that's *all* that's broken.

Rayboy   [Frightened] Stop it. *Stop it*!

Ray   Let go of me. You're frightening the boy.

Caretaker   Oh the poor little fellow . . . Come here sonny Jim.

Ray   Leave the kid alone.

Caretaker   He *made* me.

Rayboy   To *take care* . . . To *take care*.

Caretaker   [Snapping out of it] I'm sorry. [To **Rayboy**] Sorry. I don't know what came over me.

Rayboy   [To **Ray**] Are you alright?

Ray   [Snapping] *No* . . . I need a fucking drink.

Caretaker   Don't swear in front of the kid . . . Have some of this.

Ray takes a bottle from the Caretaker and swigs.

Ray   [Spluttering] It tastes like meths.

Caretaker   It *is* a bit like meths . . . Keep it. For the journey.

Ray   [Angry, shouting] I don't want you coming *anywhere* near me. Understand?

Caretaker   Yes.

Ray   So goodnight then.

Ray and the boy walk away

Caretaker   Yeah . . . Goodnight.

scene twenty-one

Ray and the boy sit down in the car park, rumble of heavy goods vehicles passing, air brakes, wheels in the rain.

Rayboy That was like my nightmares.

Ray That bleedin' Caretaker's a nightmare.
Do you collect . . .

Rayboy Moths . . . ?

Ray . . . in jam jars . . . ?

Rayboy Yes . . . The day we got the telly was Dad's most important day. I went to the railway to fill the jar with caterpillars. I was late going home and everyone was sitting in a row. There was trifle in a bowl and everyone was smart . . . and coming from the telly was the voice of a man talking all about the Princess that was going to be the Queen. The whole world was watching her turn into the Queen like she was a caterpillar inside a jar . . .

Dad threw the jam jar in the ash. He said the railway was full of murderers and not to go

back. I still went though, instead of choir.
Dad thought I was learning hymns, but I was
looking for murderers and moths . . .

There was only two people Dad liked, and one
was Stalin and one was the Queen. He *always*
sat in front of the telly, in case one of them
was on for him to watch . . .

Ray   You should draw that with your crayons.

Rayboy   You don't look very well.

Ray   A bit shaky after that scrap.

Rayboy   You've got a bloody face.

Ray   I didn't even see who did it. Apart from that
Caretaker.

Rayboy   They were *good* fighters.

Ray   Yeah, yeah.

Rayboy   They were *champions*.

Ray   It was *dark*. *Really* dark . . . What do you do
when everything is really, really dark?

Rayboy   You turn on the torch you got for Christmas
and everything goes light.

Ray   I hadn't thought of that. Look, I ought to take
       you somewhere . . . Home . . .

Rayboy No. I like doing this. With music on.

**He switches on the radio. Music plays: '*The Song is Over*'
[1971].**

Rayboy We went to see a man one day and told him
        all my dreams. 'What do they sound like?' the
        man asked, and I said, 'They sound like this'
        and sang a song. [He sings 'One Note']. And
        he caught it on the tape recorder like I catch
        the moths, quite quiet at first, the littlest of
        whispers. Then the music inside me, it got
        louder, louder, loud. And what began like
        pretty whispers turned to such great big
        music.

Ray   And he said everyone's got music in them,
        bottled up inside . . .

**A voice breaks through the music of the background
broadcast, but it is not the Hacker: it is Mary. As she
speaks Ray starts to drive faster and faster.**

Mary   [Calmly, quietly against the rhythm]
        I whisper / down the wire
        I'm invisible / I disappear

I'm a spark / Then I'm afire
I ignite / A flame of fear

Hacker [In the background] Go on . . . You're doing
good. Keep on . . . keep on . . .

Mary I heard a voice / In the night
It said 'Come to me' / Whisper low
I escape / Into the night
No goodbyes / Time to go

Hacker Listen to her speaking!

Mary Is it alright?

Hacker Yeah, yeah . . . Speak to the world.

Mary You can hear / But you can't see
I disappeared / I had no choice
I'll be a fading / Memory
I leave you this / My voice

My voice

My *voice*

Her voice echoes and builds.

**Ray jumps from station to station, searching wildly
through the channels, and then he flips. He drives faster
and faster, careening all over the road.**

Rayboy   Faster! Faster! Faster!

Ray   [Wailing] *Mary!*

And they hurtle off the motorway and crash. There is
the mangling of metal and the sound of dull collision,
breaking glass, and then eventually, silence.

scene twenty-two

The Hacker and Mary.

Hacker   Such a . . . *sweet* voice. I've *heard* that in my dreams.

Mary   Wanker.

Hacker   No! Serious. If your Dad heard that.

Mary   Oh, he'd have heard it . . . the prick.

Hacker   What did he *do* to you?

Mary   He was just a dad. You know, crap.

Hacker   What would you like to do to him?

Mary   I'd like to hurt him. I'd like to see him bleed. Why? What would you like to do to *me*?

Laughter. Kiss. Sex.

scene twenty-three

There is beautiful music, Purcell, quiet and delicate
as wings of moths. It grows and grows, and a seed of
discord is planted, which itself grows and distorts, gets
louder, twists, mutates and turns into a piercing scream
that reverberates and combines with the sound of the
manoeuvering jets. A nightmare sound of a thousand
voices screaming as Ray hurtles headlong to conscious-
ness, coming awake with a jolt amidst the mangled
wreckage of the vehicle.

Ray   Oh, God . . . Are you alright . . . ? Kid . . .
Gone. The kid has gone.

He takes out his mobile and phones Sally.

Sally   Where are you?

Ray   [Confused] We've had a bit of a scrape . . .

Sally   We?

Ray   Me and the kid.

Sally   Kid?

Ray Yeah . . . Oh, just some kid. He's gone . . .
a bump in the truck. Nothing to worry about.

Sally You've been drinking.

Ray Noo . . .

Sally Don't lie to me Ray, I know you inside out.

Ray Yes.

Sally Drunk behind the wheel . . . *Just* like old times.

Ray Listen, Sal . . .

Sally What?

Ray Mary's alive.

Sally Oh, God . . .

Ray She was on the radio . . . a poem . . . as if she
was speaking to me.

Sally Are you sure?

Ray . . . I think she's with *him*.

Sally Oh, God . . . I made myself believe that she
was dead. If she's *alive*, I have to start from
scratch.

103

Ray This world . . . [He runs out of words]

Sally Yes, Ray? This world?

Ray It's a . . . [sounding absolutely exhausted] *funny* . . . fucking . . .world.

Sally What are you going to do now?

Ray Carry on. What will you do now?

Sally [Sigh] Bake a loaf.

Ray What?

Sally I'm going to bake . . . a loaf. When you come to a place like this it's one of the things you intend to do. The rural idyll. The pine table . . . the flour and the yeast. The first born loaf. I *never* did it. And I don't know why but I'm going to bake it now. Like you said, it's a funny old world . . . *Do* phone me Ray.

Ray Yes . . .

Sally Oh, and Ray?

Ray Yes?

Sally Happy New Year.

Ray Happy what?

Sally Forget it.

Ray *If* I hear . . .

We hear a click as the phone goes dead. Song: *'Behind Blue Eyes'* [1999].

scene twenty-four

Ray starts to walk. The occasional car goes by. He sees the Caretaker up ahead, much to his dismay.

      Ray   I thought I'd seen the last of you.

Caretaker   You can't get rid of me that easy . . . Your face is a mess.

A sound of churning air grows louder as they walk. They walk amidst the noise

      Ray   Oh, shut up.

Caretaker   A windfarm! Why can't we be more like them? Beautiful giants waving at the world. A *congregation* gazing in the same direction, singing the same song.

      Ray   I am a little man amongst them. Alone. Quite, quite . . . alone.

Caretaker   Apart from me.

      Ray   Well, yes. *Apart* from you . . . God I'm drunk. How are you?

Caretaker   I am *absolutely* trashed.

Ray   And I'm bloody hungry.

Caretaker   There . . . have the last of my Burgo-Bap.

Ray   I don't want . . . Oh, listen to that *noise*. You know the weather speaks?

Music: '*Tragedy Explained*' [1999] bleeds in and out of this scene. As they listen, the windmills spin words and phrases through the air above their heads and all around them, as if words are hurtling through the heavens, mingling with the music. It is a strange and beautiful montage of sound all wrapped up in this whirling wind.

Caretaker   Strange music.

Ray   It was like my dream. When you listen closely to the beautiful music . . . the moths, the voices, the wind, the music shaped like letter 'M' birds . . . It's not beautiful. It's *not* beauty.

Caretaker   What is it?

Ray   It's a scream. The voices *scream*.

Caretaker   And the kid you used to be doesn't know . . . Where is he?

Ray   Gone back to where he belongs. Running
         home to a clip round the ear. He'll grow up
         one day and find himself sitting in a field full
         of windmills with his imaginary friend.

Caretaker   I always liked him.

Ray   You *terrified* him.

Caretaker   What?

Ray   At the services. Take-care chaps don't give
         their friends good kickings. You made him cry.

Caretaker   That was *your* fault.

Ray   My *nose* is broken.

Caretaker   [Sheepish] I didn't mean . . . I got a bit . . .
           over excited.

Ray   Well . . . now he's gone.

Caretaker   A nice kid . . .

Ray   He always liked you. Sometimes it seemed you
         were the only friend he had.

Caretaker   Yeah, well, he was lonely. Anyway: enough.
           You'll bring on the waterworks. He's far away
           from here in times gone by.

Cut to the boy.

Rayboy   After I'd been to the Middle of Nowhere to meet the man I'll one day be, I went home covered in cuts and bruises from the great big crash and Dad said, 'Who did that to you?' and I said 'The Man', and he said, 'That's your bloody lot. Get to your room!' And I went to my room and thought about all the Far Aways . . . And the biggest Far Away is where the future is, and *that's* a funny time. And I hid beneath the blankets with my torch and drew a picture of the Man all lost in that funny world . . . and I didn't want to be him any more. And I was frightened 'cos I'd seen who I would one day be, all mad and lost . . .

Cut to Mary and Hacker.

Hacker   Well, you've had your big adventure now.

Mary   [Slapping him] You cocksure *bastard*! Most people's adventures are on the telly. Telly's *crap*.

Hacker   Shouldn't be.

Mary   Dad used to work for it. He's a *pioneer* of crap.

Hacker   Doesn't *have* to be. It's in the wrong hands.

Tonight though . . . *Tonight* it's going to *happen*.
I can hear the music now. All that stuff I've
collected. Going to weave it together piece by
piece and it's gonna fill . . .

Mary The heavens!

Hacker The heavens, yeah! I'll hack it into *every* house,
fill all the tellies with the *Lifehouse*!

Mary You're . . .

Hacker *Not* mad. Come on. Get dressed.

Mary Kiss me first.

Hacker [Sharp] *Get dressed.*

Mary Where are we going?

Hacker [Sharp] Out there. Into the city. That's where
the madness is.

**And back to Ray and the Caretaker in the field of
windmills.**

Ray I think I know where Mary is.

Caretaker You've found her?

Ray   She spoke to me. On the air. She's with that
kid who hacks into the airwaves.

Caretaker   Which means you'll be going to the city?

Ray   Yeah . . . It's alright. I'm *not* going to leave you
here. We'll go together.

Caretaker   Before we go, let me give you something.

Ray   What is it? A Burgo-Bap?

Caretaker   Just something I found in the ash.

He gives him the gift.

Ray   A jam jar!

Caretaker   We'll maybe find a moth to put inside . . .

Ray   Like the old days . . .

Caretaker   Yeah, just like the old days . . .

Song: '*Behind Blue Eyes*'[1999].

**Cut to Mary and Hacker. They go down in the lift,
talking all the time. They hear voices, exaggerated
screams.**

Mary   What's that?

Hacker   Surfers. Live in the city want to go surfing, it's lifts or underground trains . . .

Mary   What?

Hacker   You should have stayed at home.

Mary   I'd have died if I'd stayed at home. All that stuff that comes down *all* the wires into *all* the rooms where *all* the people are sitting staring into *all* the screens . . . it's *all* telly.

Hacker   Might be able to coax them out. Give them something different.

Mary   What? Like the Lifehouse? When Dad was a kid he had ideas as mad as that . . . *Designing the future* . . . ! A building full of music, bright as blue Crayola. As if he could predict the future in drawings of his dreams.

Hacker   And now he grows potatoes?

Mary   A disillusioned man. It'll happen to you. The freaks are crawling out the woodwork, counting down to midnight. You'll wish you hadn't bothered.

Hacker   Are you walking or are you not walking?

Mary I'm walking.

Hacker Then you'd better keep up, 'cos if you don't, I'll slip away and you'll be lost and alone in the big, bad world.

Mary You're a patronising shit.

Hacker Yeah . . . So, *walk*.

Music: '*Who Are You*' drum loop as they enter into the city which is a mashed-up sound collage of sirens, traffic, car horns, alarms, and God knows what, all churned up into madness and spat out. Then it turns into the sound of machines.

scene twenty-five

Hinterland/slagheap. Ray and the Caretaker enter an industrial belt. The sounds of machinery mingle with music and an eerie, desolate wind.

Ray   It's like the Mountains Of The Moon.

Caretaker   Slagheaps.

Ray   When you walk through here you almost feel invisible.

Caretaker   As if all you are is a voice.

Ray   Come on, let's find her.

His voice echoes over and over again, distorts and seems to bring forth other voices.

Voices   winds
broken
lullabies
croon
sing
names

of all the disappeared
some of us
are lost
don't know
where to go
what to say
we hide
in hinterlands
become
mere memories
this is a world
where those who disappear
are yesterday's news
unless the world remembers
that they must not
forget . . .

**People emerge from trucks. There is the murmur of
voices but no direct speech. As Ray and the Caretaker
wander through the travellers' camp Ray shows Mary's
photograph to various people. There are sounds of
activity, fires, children playing, engines. We hear voices,
some in response to Ray's questions.**

Ray   Well?

Caretaker   No one's interested.

Ray   Hasn't *anybody* seen her?

Caretaker I asked everyone. On *your* behalf. No one's
seen her. You lost her. *I'm* doing my best.

Ray I've asked too. I'm doing *my* best.

Caretaker They don't trust you. *We* don't trust you.

Ray What?

Caretaker Well, all that dried blood on your face. You
look a bit weird . . . you always *were* weird.

Ray Oh, God, here we go again. Will you *shut up*.

They walk on through the camp.

Ray All these people. Why?

Caretaker They didn't want to be where they're *supposed*
to be, don't want what's on offer so they get in
their trucks and *go* . . .

Ray Last time I drove through here there was no
one. Just a huge block of concrete sticking out
of the slag. Like something off a record
sleeve. A huge, grey monolith towering
towards the sky.

Caretaker What was it?

Ray   I told myself it was a memory box.
A sarcophagus containing all the mistakes we'd
made along the way. And it would be there
long after the likes of us were dust.

Caretaker   And where is it, this tower that stands
forever?

Ray   [With a tired laugh] It isn't fucking there.

**And then as they walk, from a ghetto blaster they hear
the Hacker's voice burst out.**

Hacker   *Shout* . . . *shout* . . . *shout*. I'm *shouting* from the
rooftops . . . This is the night, the *Lifehouse
night* . . . we're gonna blow that *ento-tainment*
shit *sky-high* . . . to *kingdom come* . . . we're gonna
make the *music* of the *people* . . .

Ray   He comes in like the wind. All that stuff he
hates . . .

Hacker   . . . every pulse, every sigh, every vibration
coming together tonight and you're gonna
hear *your* music . . . *you* . . . the people who are
coming to the *Lifehouse* . . .

Caretaker   He sounds as full of strange ideas as you.

Ray   I thought all that *stuff*, the TV, the technology

... I thought it would build a congregation.
A community. I thought I could make a ...
difference.

Caretaker   [Grandly] Your *ideals* are a promise to yourself
that you break.

Ray   *He* knows what he's talking about ...

Hacker   Am I excited? Are *you* excited? I'm so excited
I feel like I'll *explode* ... What's it gonna sound
like? ... We don't *know* ...! It might be a
symphony, it might be a *cacophony* ... But it's
happening *tonight* ... and it ain't *their* music
this time ... It ... is ... *yours*! *Ours*! *Tonight* ...!
In The Lifehouse!

Ray   The world might be a better place if ...
if ...

Caretaker   If?

Ray   Yeah. The world might be a better place *if* ...
Ever baked a loaf?

Caretaker   What?

Ray   You know. A loaf. An imaginary loaf in your
case.

Caretaker   No.

Ray Then have you ever climbed a mountain?

Caretaker No.

Ray Then let's climb one. The ascent of Mount
Slagheap . . . I'll race you to the top!

He starts running up the slagheap with the **Caretaker**
puffing and panting after him. They stagger to the top
and collapse in a heap of laughter and breathlessness.

Ray *Always* climb the mountain. It's easy to forget
. . . and there it is . . .

Caretaker The *city*!

The city stretches below them. It hits them with a
collision of sheer noise, strange traffic, lost voices, grid
noise, machine hum. The beginnings of music.

Ray Come on. Let's go home.

And they walk down the hill and enter the city as the
music swells around them: '*Pure And Easy*' [1999].

scene twenty-six

City street. A cinema. They go into the cinema and we slip into the mind of the boy.

Rayboy   . . . Dad says, 'Here's some money. Run along to the flicks.' And I go like the Olympics down the High Street in the rain. The lady gives the tickets and she's gorgeous like the Queen and the Americans are silver on the screen . . .

Ray   I used to watch the heroes but they always seemed far-fetched. Rocket men with fish-bowl helmets, smiling cowboys, gentlemen of the jungle . . .

Rayboy   'Who's in the picture?' someone asks, and I say it's the Americans in the Wild West. I'm going to play them when I get home. Play Hopalong and The Man In The Mask . . .

Ray   . . . one day there was an advert in the cinema foyer - 'Caretaker Wanted'. And then I dreamed up you. A crumpled super-hero who had shadows for a home. You'd be kind –

Caretaker   – and say 'Take Care', and listen to all the things you had to say . . . And we could watch the silver screen and laugh at all the daft ideas . . .

Rayboy . . . Sometimes they put the future on and that's a proper laugh. It's all *wrong* in funny silver suits and green men in the stars. And I'm *laughing*. Laughing because I *know* about the future . . . Because I've *been*.

Caretaker A caretaker is always there when he's needed. He doesn't wear silver suits or a mask, or fly through the sky . . . he wears overalls; he's the Caretaker. He *listens*, and you and me used to sit here in the dark and watch the Rocket Man From Mars . . .

Rayboy When people ask me what the future's like, I tell them I'm *designing* it . . . And sometimes in my dreams there is a film at the Plaza called *The Boy Who Designed The Future*.

Ray And it's grey, grey, grey . . .

Caretaker Oh, please don't break my heart.

They go into the cinema and find seats. The place is half-full. The quiet murmur and gasp of a transfixed audience wraps around them in the dark.

Caretaker And which future are we watching now . . . ?

From the screen we hear the sound of screeching brakes, gunshots, shouts and cries. And then with dawning realisation Ray whispers, slowly, numbed . . .

>   **Ray** We're watching today . . . Closed circuit TV . . .
>   Edited highlights . . . Dubbed SFX . . .
>   (Christ) . . . Shopping mall kidnappings . . .
>   Building society stick-ups . . . Kerb crawlers . . .
>   Motorway pile-ups . . . Muggings . . . Tube
>   suicides . . . Prime suspects . . . Shoplifters in
>   Supermart . . . We're watching the modern
>   world . . . *This* is entertainment . . .

Music: '*Who Are You*' [Live, 1998], which shifts into Supermart muzak.

scene twenty-seven

Mary and the Hacker walking through the aisles of Supermart.

Mary   Do you always steal your food from Supermart?

Hacker   Yeah...

Mary   Oh, I get it ... You're an *outlaw*.

Hacker   Yeah.

Mary   Not exactly Billy The Kid is it?

Hacker   Look, it's time for the Lifehouse. And *if* people come ... *if* people even *talk* to each other ...

Mary   Maybe it'll just be you and me.

Hacker   And maybe there'll be thousands.

Mary   And the *music*?

Hacker   Bones, arteries, heart ... Beating out a rhythm.

Mary   A pulse . . .

Hacker   Yeah . . . What music do you think's in me?
Come on. Play the game. *If* you could hear.

Mary   I don't know . . . A beat box rhythm. A
scratched record. Boom chikka boom chikka
chik . . .

Hacker   And what's inside you?

Mary   Don't know. Some crap girl group. Some crap
song.

Hacker   But supposing we had this music inside?
Things we'd seen, places we've been. Things
we feel.

Mary   *It* might sound crap.

Hacker   It might sound beautiful.

Mary   Beautiful? Like *what?*

Hacker   Like Scarlatti.

**And Scarlatti fills the streets they walk down, beautiful
and clear. And over the music the Hacker speaks.**

Imagine if there was a place where you could

124

hear everyone's music. Imagine if they all
came together in the same place.

Mary   Yeah?

Hacker   Imagine if that place was called The
Lifehouse . . .

And the beautiful music grows.

scene twenty-eight

From Scarlatti, in sharp contrast we hear voiceover snatches. We go back to the cinema.

Ray   Mary!

Caretaker   Where?

Ray   On the screen. Not joking. With that kid. In Supermart.

Caretaker   Between soap powder and Cheesy Snax?

Ray   It's *Mary*!

Caretaker   She's a film star.

Ray   We're *all* film stars now.

He stands and heads for the exit with the **Caretaker** in tow

Ray   I think I have to leave you here.

Caretaker   I knew this was coming.

Ray   Maybe we'll meet again.

Caretaker   It was like being in a road movie.

Ray   Which one?

Caretaker   One of the Bing and Bobs.

Ray   You're ridiculous.

Caretaker   Yes . . .

Ray stops to read a poster in the foyer.

Ray   Have you read this? Listen . . . 'This cinema
will shortly be redeveloped. For the first time
ento-tainment *guarantees* spiritual growth as
well as spiritual *uplift* in a brand new *leisure
option* that will replicate the myriad dynamic
scenarios of . . . *Real Life* . . .

. . . Say 'Take care'.

Caretaker   [Quite emotional] I can't say it.

Ray   [Angry] *Say it*!

Caretaker   What will I *do*?

Ray   You're the *Caretaker*. You'll do your *duty. Say it.*

Caretaker   I am . . . *scared*. I am *nowhere* when I'm not in
your thoughts. You need me and then you
don't need me and then I am *alone*. *Fucking
alone*. Less than that . . . And *you* ask *me* to say
'Take care'?

In despair he falls silent. Ray walks away.

[Eventually. Quietly] Take care . . .

**And Ray walks into the city alone as music grows loud
all around him: *'Behind Blue Eyes'* [1999].**

scene twenty-nine

Amidst the sounds of the city, Ray's mobile rings.

Sally   You're in the city.

Ray   Yes.

Sally   And are you staying there?

Ray   Yes . . . for the time being. I don't feel far away.

Sally   You know where she is?

Ray   I saw some closed circuit footage. It *looked* like her . . . it *was* her.

Sally   Christ . . .

Ray   I've been thinking about everything. I think I got . . . I think I got so many things wrong.

Sally   I had a life in the city. I gave all that up to come to the middle of God knows where for *you* to build your dreams. I've been thinking too. Watching all the shopping channels and thinking. Thinking.

Ray Thinking what?

Sally I *know* why Mary left

Ray Why?

Sally Because . . . of . . . *you*. I should have bloody left you Ray. [Firm] She *left* because of *you*.

She hangs up. Sound of a dead line. Silence.

scene thirty

Ray starts running down the streets until he comes to an
electrical goods shop. He stands and watches the TVs in
the window display. He slugs from the bottle of booze
and shouts at all the screens.

> **Ray** Fifty telly screens and not one of you telling
> the *truth*. I told the truth. I *knew* the truth.

And he smashes the window and climbs in through the
broken glass, the security alarm colliding with the noise
from all the screens. He turns up the volume of each
one and the sound gets louder and louder. He sits
amidst the noise and broken glass, drinking and crying.
And out of the TVs comes interference, and then the
voice of the Hacker breaking in to the grid, his voice
coming through the blaring distortion of a stack of
televisions over the sound of '*Who are You*' [Live, 1998].

> **Hacker** ... *Sing* ... *sing* ... *sing* ... He's back and he's
> singing all across the sky ... I'm a voice flying
> high across the rooftops calling *you* to the mid-
> night hour ... *Nothing* can stop us now ...
> The whole *world* is waking up and walking to
> the door of the *Lifehouse* ... Who knows what

tenderness . . . regret . . . what sweet, sweet
music's gonna fill the sky tonight . . . The night
we hear the *vibrant* music of the living voice
itself . . . 'Cos this is *it* . . . This is the *Night* . . .
The Big Night . . . When all the music you've
been sending me is going to come together . . .
We're looking for one note . . . *Our* note . . .
One note and we might just change the world . . .
Tonight . . . At The Lifehouse.

Ray   I knew . . . I knew . . .

And on he walks.

scene thirty-one

Mary and the **Hacker** arrive at the Lifehouse building.
There is activity and music pulsing underneath their
voices. Song: '*Join Together*' [1999].

Hacker   The Lifehouse! This is it, then . . . what a
dream.

Mary   My Dad had dreams like you.

Hacker   What happened to them?

Mary   Other people *steal* your dreams. They get made
into television programmes.

Hacker   They can't stop it now. People are coming
from all over. The biggest thing ever.

Mary   Who *are* all these people?

Hacker   The people who send me their music. I've
collected so much stuff.

Mary   And then what?

Hacker   Feed it into the computers . . . mix it all up . . .

wait and hear what happens . . . I'm going to change the world.

Mary   *You're* going to change . . . ?

Hacker   *OK, OK, we're* going to change.

And the pulse sound swells as '*Who Are You*' [Live, 1998] drum mix bleeds in.

scene thirty-two

Ray walks into the city square. It is deserted and eerily quiet, apart from echoes of music in the distance.

> **Ray** City! Why are you whispering? Once you *roared*. You're whispering your history and there's only me to listen.

And we go to Ray as a boy. Music: Corrette.

> **Rayboy** . . . Running through the broken city thinking about the future. Dad says, 'Where've you been? You've missed another programme!' and I tell him I've been to see the man I'm going to be when I grow up. 'Oh, yes, and where's that exactly?' laughs Dad, and shakes his head. And I tell him, 'In the future. In the loneliness. In the middle of the City'.

> **Ray** City! I wonder if you remember anything that's happened in your shadows?

> **Rayboy** . . . And I tell him that I peeped from shadows into the square where the man sat and he was sitting on a television talking to the sky . . .

135

Ray City! I wonder if you can remember the small
boy living in your heart?

There is a background of beautiful, melancholy music.

Rayboy And at first I'm quite happy and the music is
all beauty . . . But when I think of the lonely
man, then the music's broken noise . . .

Ray A small boy waking and a dad listening to the
story of his dreams . . . Shaking his head like
men do who don't know *what* to do, and just
say, '*Such* funny ideas!'

Rayboy And I tell my Dad all the programmes and all
the films about the future are *wrong* stories . . .
And he tells me I'll grow up to be a man
who'll change the world . . .

Ray Oh, city! Dad told me I'd grow up to be a man
who'd change the world . . .

Rayboy And then Dad goes away. And I draw pictures
of the city *listening* to the man I'll one day be . . .
Lonely, alone . . .

Ray Once, on New Year's Eve this square would
have been full of people counting down to
midnight. Now it's full of *no*-people . . . Just
one lost soul sitting on a looted television with

nothing but a mobile phone and a . . . and a
jam jar to call his own . . .

**He doesn't know whether to laugh or cry so he does a
bit of both. And then he starts to sing a snatch of '*Too
Much*'.**

    Ray . . . I think these hands have felt a lot
            I don't know
            What have I touched.
            I think these eyes have seen a lot
            I don't know
            Maybe they've seen too much . . .

**And the recorded version [1971] takes over. Until the
end of the chorus '*Too much of everything gets too much
for me*'. Then silence.**

scene thirty-three

And then *'Baba O'Riley'* [Orchestral, 1999] begins to seep in across the rooftops and through the streets of the city replacing the eerie silence, and the voice of the Hacker echoes and spirals through the night.

> *Lifehouse*
>   *Lifehouse*
>   *Lifehouse*
>   *Lifehouse*

It repeats, mutates and reverberates through the city and Ray starts walking towards the source of the sound. We hear the boy's voice as if he is drawing the grown man's destiny. His voice mingles with the voice and footsteps of all the people who are heading towards the same place. It's as if the boy is drawing it and describing the process of drawing for us like a comic book text.

 Rayboy And out of the grey comes the bright place . . .
     The Lifehouse. And all the people are going in
     the building and all of this coloured stuff is
     the music that they hear . . .

Orchestral music comes from The Lifehouse and fills up the world. So hypnotic and so fucking beautiful that we cannot resist going in.

> Rayboy   . . . I'm using all the crayons in the box to colour in this music . . . the place is beautiful like an angel place, like a brand new sky . . . this is the man remembering music, strange like funny birds . . . *He's* got the notes inside him, and to make the music extra best . . . he's got to go inside . . .

Strange and beautiful music. Back to Ray as a man hurrying through the city.

> Ray   Mary, *Mary*!

And the people's voices mingle with the music.

> Rayboy   And all the people sound like the moths inside the jam jar . . .

Back to Ray as a man.

> Ray   Moth music, blood music, music of their hearts . . .

> Rayboy   . . . everyone's together the music grows and grows . . . and then there is just beauty . . .

everybody's stories, thoughts and dreams
come out, the sweetest sound you've *ever* heard
. . . And that's what's in my dreams, that's why
I try and draw it . . . But then because I know
the future's not a place that's full of beauty, I
take my waxy crayons and scribble the picture
out with grey . . .

Ray   When I was a small boy I used to design the
future and the picture I drew was this . . . I
heard sweet music in my dreams and *tried* to
draw the beauty that I heard. But I couldn't get
it right and so I'd make it disappear . . . the
whole world scribbled out by the hand of a
child . . . and the reason I couldn't get it right
didn't make itself clear until I was a man . . .
Because when I heard the music, when I
listened closely . . .

We hear applause, a crowd cheering.

scene thirty-four

Mary and the **Hacker** stand in the midst of the Lifehouse crowd, in the midst of the noise.

Mary   That noise . . .

Hacker   It's what it is . . . I kind of like it. Breathe . . . whisper . . . speak . . . sing . . . shout . . . scream . . . Listen to it . . . It's a busy street . . . a football crowd . . . the wind . . . ten-thousand whispers . . . it's the sea . . . Maybe it doesn't sound beautiful but I *know* it's gonna sound *huge* . . . I listen to all that and I think . . .

Mary   What do you think?

Hacker   I think *anyone* who wanted to could blow this place away.

Mary   [Aghast] Why?

Hacker   Chemistry. Alchemy . . . !

Mary   [In disbelief] No one would really do that?

Hacker   Oh, but they would.

Mary   Who?

Hacker   Someone in that crowd. Someone like you.
Maybe we'll all make it happen but we won't
know we've done it. Magic. Good stuff . . .
bad stuff. Good people. Bad people. Mixing
up. 'Cos this is The Lifehouse and maybe it's
all gonna blow.

Mary   What?

Hacker   [Quietly] boom

**There is an earth-shattering explosion and The
Lifehouse blows sky high. And then there is deathly
silence save for sirens and alarms in what's left of the
city night.**

scene thirty-five

Ray walks into the ruins of the house that he was born in, where a bonfire flickers and crackles. The sirens in the night are far away and a clock bell chimes.

> Ray   Back to where everything started. Back to the ruins of the house where I was born.

He sits down amidst the rubble and sighs.

> Ray   [Quiet] Mary.

We go back to Ray as a boy. We can hear his crayons moving across paper.

> Rayboy   This is a picture of a nightmare . . . This is the man who is sad and afraid and alone sitting in front of a television on fire . . . This is a sadness . . . This is the man's lost daughter . . . This is the man seeing her through some tears because he thought she'd gone forever . . . This is my big black crayon and this is me scribbling all over the picture and making the man's daughter disappear into the sky and into

space all gone goodbye . . . This is blowing up.
Boom! Blowing up. Boom. This is the sad man
screaming.

Ray   No. Mary. No.

Rayboy   Screaming forever.

Ray   *No. Mary. No . . .*

Rayboy   This is a warning.

Ray   *No.*

Rayboy   This is the future.

scene thirty-six

Ray   I feel like the man in one of my waxy pictures whose life's been scribbled away.

Rayboy   Look at the man in all his tears like a man in a black sea, drowning.

Ray dials home on his mobile. We hear the tone.

Ray   Pick up, Sal . . . *Pick up*!

Rayboy   Nothing.

And then we hear the computerised operator.

Voice   The number you have dialled has *not* been recognised . . .

Rayboy   Nearly silence.

Voice   Please replace the handset and try again . . . The number you have dialled . . .

He throws the mobile on the fire.

Rayboy All . . . alone.

**Sound of a city. Voice repeating, mingling with
Rayboy's voice 'Alone . . . Alone . . .' Ray sobs.
Voices twist and fade. Rayboy sings *'One Note'*,
then *'Baba O'Riley'* [Orchestral, 1999] plays under
the credits.**

End